Bigfoot Boy - Lost on Earth

Bigfoot Boy

\-

Lost on Earth

Kenna McKinnon

To my children

The author acknowledges the skill and friendship of Judith Hansen, who initially edited this novel and saw it through from conception to completion.

It was Judi's suggestion of a story about a Sasquatch alien teen that prompted this novel in the first place.

I would like to thank Miika and Petteri and the staff at Creativia for their kind acceptance of Bigfoot Boy, the wonderful new cover, and the opportunity to bring it to the light of day once again.

I am very grateful to my family, children, and friends for their support and unconditional encouragement of my writing career.

Not least, I acknowledge the early start our parents gave us as they encouraged me to read voraciously and precociously, and write from a very early age.

In particular, professors at the University of Alberta taught me to think, and for that I will always be grateful.

Chapter One

"Errl. Pssst. Look at this. It's ill," Errl's best friend Berndt whispered. "The humans eat *eggs*. They're camping right below. Something is sizzling in a flat iron pan. Worm infested pig meat and eggs. Gross."

"Shut up. The Teach is looking at us."

"Dr. Teach? He's too touched to notice."

"He thinks out loud same as us. Gummy wad, Berndt?"

"No, thanks. My cud's full."

The boys and girls with big hairy feet were on their yearly field trip to Earth from Planet X. Errl, the smallest of them, combed the hair on his legs. He didn't want to listen to their MiddleSchool teacher. They were learning English and Errl heard enough to get by if he had to. Getting by was good enough for him. Later he wished he had listened more carefully.

"Shhh. Some cute girls just got on the airpod."

"Where?"

"Oh, that's your sister, Errl. Torannee. Hard to tell with the long blue streaked hair down the front."

"Ee-yah. All the girls are coloring their body hair now."

"Still. Your sister's cute, Errl."

Their speech sounded like grunts and bleeps to an untrained ear. Even by Bigfoot standards, Errl was ugly. He began to comb the hair on his face.

"Gross. Who's her friend?"

"I think it's Lally. I wish Teach hadn't kept the girls in another part of the ship. It's hard to tell one from the other." Berndt flattened his webbed fingers and whistled. "There's water down below." He scanned the Moduports in the front of the airpod. Teach grunted into the control panel. The pod eased across the tops of the forest below, scaring deer into the open. Their ship was silent and still, invisible to the group of young human campers.

"They're eating eggs and wormy pork meat, with chunks of rat infested bread."

"Ee-yah, their eyes and smell aren't as keen as ours, Errl. The rest of us, anyhow. Maybe not you." Berndt laughed. He slapped Errl on the back.

Errl put down the comb. Teach dropped his gummy wad. He picked it up again and chewed. Errl's sister smiled at Berndt behind her long blue hair.

"What's that white stuff on the big hills?"

"They call it winter. Don't you know nuffin'?" Berndt winked at the six feet tall Bigfoot girl. She was starting to show signs of stars in her eyes and long hair on her belly.

"I'd rather sleep than listen to Dr. Teach."

The ship lurched. Teach went skidding past them. The laser machine that guided the airpod sparked and smoked. The girls clung to the rails at the side. They tried to get to the control panel. Lally whipped her long arms around the controls and pulled. Teach skidded past them again as the ship righted itself. Errl grasped the rails. The ship screamed to an emergency landing in the forest below, Torannee and Lally at the controls. Teach grunted and swore. His fuzzy hair matted where he sat on his butt.

"Holy pine nuts," Errl said. "What happened, Dr. Teach? The Humans must have seen that."

"One of their radio satellites knocked out our power," Teach said. "I forgot to set the screens."

"You *forgot* to set the screens?"

"No harm done," Torannee said. "The human campers didn't see us." Her voice sounded like sacks of rocks crunching together. Berndt thought she was beautiful.

"I don't think they saw us, anyhow."

She was wrong.

The rest of the Bigfoot boys crowded into the cockpit. "Are we really going out now, Teach?" they asked. "Can we stay a while and wade in the water that's white capped over there, frozen in places? We're so hot in this cabin, Teach."

"Not now, boys." The MiddleSchool teacher brushed himself off and rose to his feet. He regained his dignity. He adjusted the thick vision aids on his flat nose and secured them with hair from his face.

"When are we going out?"

"Our big ship is circling their moon. We'll have to meet up when it gets here."

"We can't stay in the pod, Dr. Teach. It's getting way too hot in here."

"Yes, they'll have to send another pod to rescue us. Wait, boys and girls. Have a fresh gummy wad and I'll try to pry the door open."

Lally's hairy hand moved and pulled a lever. The door swung open.

"Yay!" Six Bigfoot boys seven feet tall poured out of the open door, followed by the two girls. Errl wasn't as tall as the rest of his friends. His eyes were weak and he blinked in the bright sun. His sister hung behind with Berndt.

"The river!" They dashed to the edge of the roaring water. White caps foamed on top. Bits of ice floated down stream. The forest was on the side of a mountain.

"Where's the humans?" Errl asked.

"I didn't see them again," Berndt said.

"Where's my gummy wad?" Teach adjusted his vision aids. He chewed on a fly that was hung up in his body hair.

The boys leaped into the river. Errl hung back at the shore. He didn't like water.

"What's the matter, Teacher's boy, you loser? Don't want to get *wet*? Your Mam didn't raise no Bigfoot athlete?"

"I'll be with you in a nanosecond." Errl looked at Teach. Teach held a small box in his hairy hands. He signaled the big ship 238,000 miles away.

The airpod smoked and flames began to flicker from inside.

"We're going to set fire to the forest." The boys splashed in the river and put distance between themselves and the pod.

"Torannee, what do we do?"

The girl with the blue hair ran back inside the pod and threw open a cupboard. She took out a hose. Thick foam gushed into the pod. The fire went out. The ship smoked.

"It's useless," Teach said, brushing himself. "We have to wait for the big ship."

"When?" Errl asked. He put a toe in the frozen water.

"They'll be here at six chronos."

"That long?"

"Well, they're hanging out at the Earth moon. There's junk on the moon. They want to clean it up first and put up our flag."

"That's more important than keeping us safe?"

"Every year we come here on our field trip to learn more about Earth. We have to be secret. Earth people don't like strangers. Nobody knows what happens on their moon."

"I think they do," Torannee said. She smiled and stroked the blue hair on her belly. From the river, the boys whistled and yelled.

"They do, don't they, Teach?" Errl asked.

"Some of them do. But our Bigfoot are very smart. Our flag looks like what the humans call a hammer and sickle. They'll blame the Russians."

"They're still fighting the Russians?" Lally asked, who had studied MiddleSchool Earth history.

"No. That's why we're so smart. There won't be a war. They'll just yell at each other."

"Why don't we put up another flag and leave the junk there? What do we care?"

"Our captain has a sense of humor. He's also a dirt disturber."

4

"Oh," Torannee said and waved at Berndt in the river.

"Can I go for a walk in the forest, Teach?" Errl asked. *I don't like water. And I have to relieve myself. The farther away I get from these smart alecks the better I'll like it. I like games. If I hide in the forest they'll have to look for me. What fun!*

"Yes, I suppose so, but be back by six chronos. We must leave then. Don't be late. We'd have to leave you behind, Errl, if you're not here then. The new airpod will have to meet the ship at a certain spot in the sky. We can't be late. The big ship will be in orbit. If you're not here at six chronos it will be another ten loops of the moon around the Earth again before we can come back to look for you. Our instruments were set on our Planet before we left. We can't differ."

"I understand, Teach." Errl glanced at the chronometer on his arm. He grunted and loped into the forest.

He did not have a good sense of direction. On Planet X he depended on his friends to find the long way back to his home and parents after a week of MiddleSchool. On a field trip he was almost useless.

It's so dark here in the forest. I smell strange animals and their droppings. It wipes out the smell of the river. Everything looks the same. I don't know where the sounds are coming from. Strange sounds and smells are all around me. Where am I?

Dr. Teach shouldn't have let Errl go into the forest alone. The big brown trunks of the fir trees closed around the boy and his weak eyes blinked in the dim light. Errl walked farther and farther from the river.

Be back by six chronos? Darn frog's foot, I forgot to bring my tech compass.

The trees loomed over his head. His hairy broad feet tripped on roots and shrubs. The gloom of the forest closed around him. He no longer knew the direction of the downed and smoking pod. He heard only the buzzing of insects and the wind through the tops of the trees.

On and on he stumbled. *This isn't a game anymore*, he thought. He was lost.

Chapter Two

The forest was a scary place. On Errl's home Planet X there were no trees. Just wide spaces with tall grass, shrubs, lakes, huge buildings and airships in the sky.

I see why we visit Earth. So much to see that's strange. So much to learn. By Zorster's toenails, I need my gummy wad.

What's that?

Huge dark firs blocked his path. A small creature with a bushy tail ran up a tree.

The creature has a nut in its paws, like the Krakzen nuts at home that grow on shrubs. The nuts are good to eat. My gummy wad is gone. I missed the last meal. The creature must give me its food.

The creature chattered and ran higher as Errl began to climb the tree and came to the first branch. He crawled out on the branch as far as he could. The creature looked at him with sharp bright eyes. It smiled.

Give me your food. I'm hungry. Errl didn't think that he could gather nuts by himself.

He had to learn to think for himself. This was his first lesson. He slept or talked through most lessons.

You little Krakzen thief. Give me that.

The branch broke as Errl reached out for the bright eyed creature. The creature leaped to the next branch and chattered at him. The Bigfoot boy dropped to the ground.

Falling straight to the forest floor, he realized that at almost seven feet and four hundred pounds, he was lucky. Lucky and strong. Still, it was a horrible fall and when he hit the soft pile of leaves, he felt a tree root crack.

He lay in the pile of dead leaves and frozen mud.

Oh, my sore back. What happened? Where am I? Am I okay? Are my bones broken? Is anything broken? Did someone hear me fall? Ugh. Ugh. Help! Help! He lay flat on his back and snorted and coughed. The humans half a mile away heard him fall and heard him call out. The leader cocked his gun.

The creature tried to kill me. The animal with the bushy tail ran all the way up to the top of the fir. It looked down at him and chattered. It dropped the nut in its paws. The nut fell on his face and bounced off his receding chin. He felt his ribs.

Nothing broken, maybe. I am huge strong Bigfoot.

The nut rolled away on the rocky forest floor, bounced through the dead leaves and settled next to a root. He sat up.

I feel pretty foolish. If Berndt could see me now he would laugh. I'm glad Lally can't see me. She would laugh, too. They would think I'm a fool.

Yes, he was a fool. He reached for the nut and cracked it against his knee, breaking it open. Putting it in his mouth, he was surprised it tasted so good. He looked up at the bushy tailed animal. He was convinced the furry being looked down at him and laughed. He could almost hear its thoughts.

Foolish alien Bigfoot boy.

Errl began to laugh along with bushy-tail. He sounded like a moose calling its mate.

Here, get another nut for me, my little pet.

The squirrel ran to the end of a branch and jumped to another tree. Errl watched it go. Why couldn't *he* gather food? Did all food have to come from a *compukitchen*?

No, he could gather food. Dr. Teach had taught them about cooking. What did the teacher say again?

On Earth you will gather fruit, berries and other plants for research. You can eat the plants that will not hurt you. How do you know? Look at this chart. I'll teach you what plants you can eat, what plants you should gather for research, what plants to stay away from, like these stinging plants that will hurt you.

Stinging plants. Your thick coats will protect you. But don't pick the stinging plants with the soft palms of your hands and don't eat them.

What stinging plants? He looked around. Then he looked down. What he had thought was a soft bed of leaves was something else.

It was green and the leaves were pointed and covered with fine hairs.

A stinging plant.

The squirrel looked at him from another tree top and laughed.

I must find something to eat. Bigfoot boy scratched his bottom. That was a mistake. The palms of his hands burned. He had no medicine. What had Dr. Teach said?

Find some mud and put it on the sting. Let it dry. It will take the sting out.

Mud. The ground was hard and cold. How do you make mud? He scratched his head, which was sore where the hair was thin on his forehead.

I need some water and dirt to make mud.

He got slowly to his feet. His body hurt but he shook himself. He was strong and he figured he wouldn't hurt for long.

His face and the palms of his hands burned. He looked around. There were patches of what his Teach called snow on the ground, mixed with dead leaves and spongy green stuff. He began to think for himself.

I'll mix my hands around in this snow and it will melt because I'm hotter than the snow. It will mix with the dirt and the leaves and this green spongy stuff. It already feels better.

He made a big mess of wet leaves and mud, packing it onto his hands and forehead. He was a very strange looking big footed alien. The sting went away, though. He threw back his head and roared. He was very proud of himself. He had solved his first puzzle in the wilds of Earth, without his Teach or Berndt or his sister to tell him how.

Not knowing which way to go, Errl continued to walk. Often he looked at his chronometer. It was close to the time his ship would send another airpod to rescue them. He would miss the ship. He would have to stay here for another ten lunar passes around the Earth. Then another airpod would come with the big ship. He didn't want to wait that long, unsure if he could remember where to catch it if it came again. Teach had said it would come again if he missed this one. Teach never lied. *Did he?*

As his Kinfolk felt when they were hurt or tired, Bigfoot boy was hungry and beginning to feel cold. He walked and walked. He didn't hear the shouts of his classmates and Teach. He had keen hearing, but he had walked too far, and the wind was too loud in the trees. He heard another sound, too.

It was not the sound of the river.

There was also a smell which he had only sensed when they were above the Human camp, hovering around its edges. He peered with his poor eyes through the trunks of fir trees, in a direction he thought he had walked already from the downed pod. He must go back. Danger was here in the forest.

Again he looked again at his chronometer. Six chronos. Oh, Zorster's demons and bells, he was late! He began to run toward the setting yellow sun. He thought, *If I run without thinking I'll be in trouble.* He stopped every now and then to look and listen.

Then he saw it on the path in front of him. He slowed and stopped and stared. The animal looked back.

Chapter Three

What are you? Black fur, brown nose, four legs like the stumps of trees. You snuffle and eat dry red berries from the bushes at the side of the trail. I've seen you before, on our telescreens in MiddleSchool.

Bear. No danger.

Good fellow.

The bear growled at him and lunged.

I'll share your berries.

Errl began to run. Through the firs, crashing over fallen logs, through bogs of wildflowers, the bear behind him.

Grrrrr.

Holy Zorster's demons and bells, the thing was fast! Little blue pockets of snow crushed beneath his feet as he ran. He jumped over broken branches and fallen logs, running *away* from his ship. He threw a glance over his hairy shoulder and then leapt in another direction. The bear followed, zig-zagging through the forest. They were at an angle to the ship, as far as Errl could tell, but he had lost all sense of direction.

He tripped on a root and fell.

The black bear pelted by him, stopped and came back. Errl lay on the ground and groaned. He tried to get up but the bear held him down with one huge paw.

I'm doomed.

The bear began to sniff him.

The smell is familiar. She smells like Dr. Teach.

The bear began to lick him all over, from his hairy moist face to his chest, down the side of his bleeding and bruised body, to his legs and feet.

She thinks I'm a cub.

Where did the thought come from? He didn't know, but remembered a classroom one warm day, Teach droning at the back of the room. The telescreens had been alive with Earth information and had prepared him for this day, lost on Earth.

Next she'll see I'm not a cub. What then?

With a quick look, he searched for a branch to use as a club. He lay with one arm twisted under him. He was big and strong and might be able to fight this bear. First he would see if it was a threat. So far the bear licked him and growled and then...

A sound in the forest beside them. Through the bushes, Errl could see a flash of golden fur, a tall broad form something like himself...a Bigfoot girl like Lally but much smaller. He felt shame for being on the ground, needing help, meeting a strange Earth creature like himself for the first time, like this. He was big and strong. He was a boy. He would protect her, the golden creature.

She reached down and grasped a fallen log in both hands, raised it high.

No, don't hit me.

The log crashed down on the bear's neck. The unconscious animal sprawled across Errl's chest. It snorted in shallow breaths and Errl pushed it to one side and got to his feet.

"Stop. Come back. Don't run."

The girl didn't understand his language. She ran through the trees and was gone. She smelled like woodbine and crushed cattails. He knew from the telesensors in class the smells of Earth, when he had paid attention. He liked the smell of woodbine—honeysuckle was sweet.

Will I see you again? Come back.

She had saved his life. She was brave as his sister, Torannee. He felt his own ugliness. The bear lay on the forest floor and Errl nudged it with his foot. The bear lumbered to its feet and ran off. Errl laughed.

Brave Bigfoot girl.

The golden girl was gone. Was she real?

Pretty girl. Nice girl. He began to run back along the same path on which he'd met the bear. The berries were still there, dry and covered with frost, the bushes crushed. He began to eat the berries.

Good berries. They'll be better in the summer of this planet, but they're good now. I was very hungry. It takes a lot to fill up a Bigfoot boy.

Not a bad bear. Now where had Errl been going in such a hurry? His chest hurt. His feet were bruised. Oh, yes.

The ship. I'm late.

He broke into a trot. He knew he would never get there on time. What had his friends said?

You're a loser, Errl.

Yes, he was. He was a loser and he couldn't help anyone else. He couldn't help the golden girl. He couldn't help himself. The girl had saved him and he hadn't even thanked her. Like his sister, she was stronger and smarter than him. Who wasn't?

Looking around, Errl strained to hear the sounds of his friends calling him from the ship far away, but all he could hear was the wind soughing through the treetops. Their craft would leave without him. He would be alone on this strange planet for ten more days, if he could get back then. If he could remember where he left the ship.

His heart pounded like the engine of an airpod. The cold wind whipped by his flattened ears and he was frightened. The bear hadn't scared him. The fall from the tree hadn't scared him.

But he was afraid to be alone, and he began to run very fast farther into the forest.

Chapter Four

I'm only thirteen Earth years old. Though Bigfoot boys act older than Earth years, I'm too young to be alone on a strange planet. They'll leave without me, I know they will. Teach said they would. I don't know where I am. My chronograph says it's almost time to leave. Maybe I can signal if I see the new airpod coming in? It's invisible and silent to humans but I can see it. I can hear it. There, is that it?

Errl stood for a minute in the forest, a hunched brown furry figure. A cold wind screamed in his ears and hid the sound of distant shouting. High above the forest a yellow sun moved through the clouds. The clouds were heavy with snow. He felt good in the cold air, his thick mat of body hair shielding him from the cold. The bear was long gone and the girl just a memory. He felt cold only if he was sick. He thought, *I am strong. I am not a loser. I will remember what I was taught. My MiddleSchool was a good school. Nobody in MiddleSchool is a loser.* Except maybe Errl.

Which way should I turn? Every direction looks the same.

If he could find the river he could find the crashed pod, Dr. Teach and his friends. This time their research field trip to Earth had gone horribly wrong.

A shadow passed over the cold yellow sun. He looked up. The tops of the trees whipped in the wind. He thought he could hear running water far away.

Why did I walk so far? I wanted to be alone. Teach was driving me pine nuts. By Zorster's armpits, I don't belong with those guys, anyhow. I'm such a failure. Berndt and my sister were ignoring me. Lally is so cute but she makes me uncomfortable. The others were razzing me. I don't like water. I'm not like them. I'm ugly. I'll always be different. Why did I leave home to go on this darn trip, anyhow?

He was lost, but he was thinking, and he still had hope.

Just a nanomoment. What direction does the Earth sun rise? He couldn't remember. Teach had covered that in class yesterday. He had been grooming himself, chatting to Berndt, nodding off in the warm room.

Then he saw it. He was too late.

A shadow passed over the sun. There was a whoosh of hot air from the sky. The grey oval of an airpod sank on the other side of the firs and shrubs. Between him and the rescue ship was a mile of woods, tangled roots and shrubs white with frost.

Waving and shouting, suddenly he remembered the young campers they had spotted on their way down. He skirted the area where he had seen them and closed his mouth. Other trips had taught the Bigfoot not to mess with humans. Humans had fierce animals at their disposal to hunt down the Bigfoot, long sticks which spewed fire like lasers, cells in which they kept the fiercest creatures they knew.

I'd be lucky to be put behind those bars in a cell with rotten food, and not killed first with no questions.

He ran faster in the direction where he'd seen the airpod put down. It was hidden behind tall firs and dense shrubs.

I'll never make it.

As all Bigfoot knew how to do, he ran smoothly and fast. He covered ground in easy loping strides. Then the sun went behind a cloud again. His sense of direction wavered.

Where did I hear the airpod? Where did I see it put down?

Stopping, he looked around. Every direction looked the same.

Why didn't I pay more attention in class?

Then he heard the familiar whoosh of hot air and saw the same shadow cross the sun. The airpod was rising toward a huge shape in the sky which opened and swallowed it as he watched. The big ship vanished. It moved so fast back into orbit that now it was a dot in the sky and then...nothing.

He stood in abject misery.

Useless. I'm useless. I've missed my ride.

It was hopeless. They wouldn't be coming back for another ten lunar passes around the Earth. Tied into their travel system and loyal to their government on Planet X, the papers the captain signed before they left, and the other students Dr. Teach was responsible for—the adult Bigfoot had left him holding a bag of mealy worms. Fear coursed through his body.

He could hear a crackle of steps in the woods behind him. If it were one of the furry animals on Earth, he could hold his own. But it sounded like a group of Humans, and they were coming closer. The sound was like feet crunching on dry frozen twigs. Or it could have been a hammer cocking on a fire stick that spit death.

I don't want to find out.

He ran away from the sounds, but he wasn't lucky. He burst through an opening in the woods and stood face to face with the young human campers and their leader.

Chapter Five

"Holy brown sugar. What is that thing?" The older man in front stood as tall as Errl's shoulder. Except for a patch of fur on his upper lip, the strange fellow was hairless and white. Errl stared at him and the man stared back. The children were dressed in blue shirts and brown hats. They had small rocks in their hands. The taller man wore a brown shirt and jeans, and a funny hat. Errl smiled and waved his arms in the Bigfoot gesture of peace.

I give up. The sounds came out like a growl. He spread his lips wide and bared his teeth. *My ship left without me.* He made smacking noises with his lips and tried again to smile.

"D-d-don't come any closer, mate." The man held a small metal object in his hand. It looked like a thing to talk into, Errl thought.

The boys and girls moved back. One of the bigger boys began to cry. Someone screamed.

Don't be scared of me. Errl threw his arms about in a gesture of peace.

"Don't you dare come any closer, you furry beast. I'll blow your head off."

The tone of his voice doesn't sound safe. Not for me. Not for his little friends. What should I do? Bigfoot boy tried to think what his Mam would tell him to do. He tried to think what Dr. Teach would say, or Berndt. His sister would tell him to kick the guy's belly and run.

What is that metal thing? It gleams in the sun. The man took a small smooth square out of the blue cloth that covered his chest and spoke into it.

Ah. That's a thing to talk into. They had one of those in the ship. He wished he had one now. He would call his Teach and ask him what to do.

The shiny metal thing was pointed and ugly. The leader waved it in one hand, held the smooth square with the other hand.

I don't know what you're saying to me. I don't have my Teach who speaks your language. I didn't do my class work.

Errl was becoming upset, baring his teeth and trying to smile. He waved his arms in peace. Snow began to fall and turned his brown hairy body white. The leader took a step forward and put his pink face into Errl's field of vision. The children screamed and began to run away. Errl grunted and screamed, too.

The man cried, "Stop!" and fired his gun.

Later, Errl thought he had stared death in the face and won. Later, he knew enough to stay away from humans with guns. He knew enough to stay away from the Cub leader. He remembered now what the man and the kids were. Teach had went over it with them, saying they could be anywhere in the woods at any time. The leader had seen the airship go down and guessed Errl was an alien. The Cub leader hated him. He hated aliens. Earth was not safe for Errl. He must run and keep on running until he reached a safe place.

He never knew how he got from the clearing in the forest to the woods so fast. The forest was quiet. Snow didn't reach the ground. It melted on the tree tops. He brushed himself off and tore like Zorster's demons through the trees. He tripped on roots and shrubs as he ran, branches whipped his face.

Am I alive? Did he hit me? Am I bleeding?

All Bigfoot people knew how to swim. Errl didn't like water, but he was a Bigfoot teen and he knew how to swim, so he ran for the river. He could swim away from the scary man and his gun. The man was talking on the smooth square thing to other humans, Errl knew. Soon there would be more.

There'll be more shots fired, and they will try to kill me. Worse, they might take me to a cell and then cut me up with a knife to find out what is a Bigfoot man. I heard that. It happened before. Humans caught Bigfoot cousins.

Nasty, nasty humans.

Am I alive? Am I bleeding? He kept on running. He could hear the river through the woods. It was wild, white capped, rough, and bits of ice were swirling downstream.

Errl didn't stop to think about what he was doing. Another shot rang out behind him. Both shots had missed. He might not be so lucky next time. He knew what a weapon was, and what it could do.

Bigfoot adults on my Planet X don't always live in peace, just like this small human with a big gun. I come in peace, human. You didn't listen to me.

He couldn't know that his speech sounded harsh and dangerous to human ears. He couldn't know that his gestures of peace looked like a threat. His large hairy body wove in and out of the trees, blending into the shadows. He ran without a sound on padded feet. At the riverbank he didn't stop to think. He took a breath and dived into the cold water, pulled down by the current too swift for him to swim away. How could he have known the river would rise and take with it pieces of ice, white caps, logs, sticks, roll rocks at the edge of the water, and drag him with the current downstream?

I wanted to swim across the river. I can't, I can't, I'm being pulled along. Help me, Mam, Teach, little sister, Berndt. My head's going under, I can't breathe, my lungs are full of icy water, I'm cold and the human is chasing me along the banks, shooting at me... He was swept into the middle of the flood. Bullets whined over his head. Finally, the man turned back. Errl continued to fight the current as he was swept downstream in the icy grip of winter in the Kootenays.

Colder than Planet X. Colder than our poles. I am going to die.

Night pulled a black curtain over his eyes. The river became rougher. The water coursed along at punishing speed. He was bashed by rocks; fell hundreds of feet over a cliff of water. He bobbed silently in a pool at the bottom of the waterfall, battered by currents, battered by rocks and logs which fell with him. Battered and bloody and bruised.

Choking, shivering, coughing up water, he dragged himself from the pond at the edge of the whirlpool. His hands slipped on icy rocks. His hair was matted and bloody. He staggered to the shore.

Far away, he could hear the sound of barking animals and men's voices. He dug himself a hole in the frozen mud in the riverbank, covered himself up with fallen rotted leaves, crawled as far as possible from sight behind a wall of driftwood and old logs. The voices came closer.

Can they see me? Can the zammots *smell me? I can smell them, wet hairy dogs like the bear. Want to bite me. I will bleed more and they will find me. Teach said the Humans use dogs to find us. I'm so cold and wet. If I'd gone in the river with Berndt and my friends I wouldn't be here now. I could have played in the river with my friends. I like to play games better than listen to Dr. Teach. That's why I'm here. That's why I'm in trouble. I wanted to see what was in the forest. I should have stayed in the MiddleSchool group. They listened to Teach. This isn't a game. Errl is so wet and hurt.*

Oh, why is Errl such a loser?

No, I am not a loser. I am a Bigfoot boy who will get back home. This is an adventure. I will sleep now and it will be better in the morning. Maybe in the morning I will meet a friend. *This isn't a game.*

Chapter Six

The riverbank was alive with sounds. Errl awoke at midnight, groggy and dazed. Where was he? He was cold. The sounds of men and dogs had faded away for the night. Other sounds took their place.

Teach. What did you teach us about the creatures on Earth? Which ones will hurt us and which are harmless? I wish I had paid more attention in class.

Frogs. "By all frogs' feet and snapping turtles" was a popular thing to say in his Earth exobiology class. That meant they covered river life in exobiology lessons. So what about it?

No, I can't eat frogs or snapping turtles. Ugh. Bigfoot don't eat meat. That is so ill, Berndt would say, and I agree. I can't eat frogs or swimming things or anything from this river. But what of the plants? Teach said seaweed is very good. Humans eat it. Is there seaweed on this riverbank?

From his little nest in the bank, he looked around. There were black strands of something slimy caught on the logs. He was sure that would be good to eat. He reached out and tried to taste what he thought were plants.

Farther up on the bank he could see cones, too, and more of the nuts lying on the ground like the bushy tailed creature had thrown at him. He got out of his cave. The slimy stuff tasted ill, but it was a lot like cooked *Okeree* and he swallowed it. It stayed in his stomach. Some cones had tumbled to the bottom of the riverbank. He crunched on them, and they were good, especially the nutty centers of the cones.

He wandered about in the dark, slurping up weeds, algae, crunching on pine cones and nuts.

This place is a little compukitchen. He was very proud of himself. He was looking after himself out in the wilds of Earth with no one to tell him what to do. He thought hard. He tried to remember what Teach said in exobiology class. Mostly things about Humans and other animals. Teach said every year the Bigfoot came to Earth in a different place that was out of the way, and they stayed out of sight of Humans.

But Teach taught us how to live if we got lost.

He thought hard. When he wasn't in MiddleSchool he lived with his Mam and Pa in a very high building near a large lake. There were plants near the lake, plants strange to Earth but familiar to him, blue and purple and red plants, plants with huge yellow stamens and stalks ten feet high, plants that were good to eat, fruits and corn and tubers and starches, all of which his Bigfoot Kinfolk ate from the compukitchens. The robots prepared the food and the Kinfolk ate it. It was not often his Mam and Pa allowed him to go out on his own and gather food for himself, although it was available.

The wars made the city not safe.

He welcomed the yearly trip on the huge ship to alien planets like Earth. He didn't have to think about war or laser shooting or...

Had he seen a fire stick Teach had told them about? An Earth gun that would wound and even kill a Bigfoot? Because Teach said there were other Bigfoot here on Earth, the Kinfolk must not touch them or teach them. They had come to Earth a long time ago and were not like the Kinfolk. They must be left alone.

Humans shot at Bigfoot on Earth, Teach said. They would shoot his Kinfolk, too. That was why the big ship was invisible and silent to Human ears and eyes. Only a few of the small airpods could be seen, without screens, too small for screens. The airpods were fast and could get away fast, too. His airpod had crashed and he knew the Captain would beam it up before the Humans could find it. That meant there was only one way off Earth. They would have to send another airpod. *And soon,* he thought, *I don't know if I can survive on Earth much longer.*

There was no moon tonight. The riverbank was black and dangerous. His poor eyes could not see far but he saw farther than the Humans could. He saw the churning waterfall he had fallen down last night. He saw the eyes of animals in the forest behind him. He heard the roar of the river and the quiet of the pool here at his feet. He shivered and thought, *the sound of the crashing water would hide the sounds of someone following me.*

Then he pulled the leaves over himself again in his little mud cave in the side of the riverbank. The stars swung cold and bright behind a blanket of cloud. There was no moon. He was warmer in the cave covered by leaves. Far away the hounds bayed and someone shouted. There were lights far up the river, but he felt safe.

Chapter Seven

The single yellow sun on this planet was so bright. It hurt Errl's eyes when he stumbled out of his makeshift mud cave in the morning and blinked at the forest surrounding him.

I'm cold. He shivered and hopped from one big hairy foot to the other, looking about him. Last night he had heard dogs and men. Hunting him.

Where are they now?

He drank from the river, then began to claw his way up the riverbank. He slipped more than once, held onto rotting roots and uplifted logs, skinned his knees on sharp wet rocks. At last he stood at the top of the bank.

What now, Teach? Where are you, Berndt? My eyes hurt and I'm hungry.

He began to lope amongst the columns of fir trees and cypress, stumbled in the underbrush, face whipped by branches and feet crunching on frozen cones. He looked up.

An eagle circles overhead. I know the bird from my exobiology books. I'm too big for him now, but if I fall...? I'm bleeding. I'll lead animals of prey to me, like the sharks in the oceans here, hungry for my blood. I'm weak. I must find shelter and better food.

The eagle circled, a bird of prey. Something rustled in the forest ahead of him and his ears were keen. He heard the rodents under cover of the frozen grass, heard something larger moving away a few yards from the river bank, heard the splash of fish in the river behind him.

What's that? Through the trees?

He pushed his bleeding face through an opening in the forest. He saw a cabin sitting in a ray of sun. Made of logs, with a single dirty window and a plank door.

*What day is it of this new world? When do my Kinfolk come back to get me? Teach said... ten loops of the moon around this earth. How long did I sleep? What day is it today? They'll be back at six chronos on the tenth day...*he checked his chronometer. Time was so different here on this new planet Earth. The sun whirled in the too blue sky, the sun too bright, the sky too blue.

Striding to the cabin, Errl pushed on the door. It gave easily to his broad shoulder and he crashed into the small room.

The room was deserted. *Good. Now food? Some human lived here, not here now. Where's food? I'm hungry. Teach, Berndt, did my sister make it to the airship? What about Lally? Will they come back for me?*

Yes, there's food here.

There were cans with pictures on them, and when he rummaged through a drawer he found a tool that might open a can. The tool was sharp on one end, blunt on the other. It also would make a good weapon, he thought.

Attacking a can with the tool, it slipped and cut his thumb.

Zorster's hairy ears, that hurt.

His third try was successful. He dumped something brown and lumpy into a dish and spooned it into his mouth. He knew the Humans ate meat, and thought, *thank Zorster, this isn't flesh.* Or eggs.

He read the label. B-E-A-N-S.

Whatever it is, I'm not hungry anymore. He burped and farted.

A cot with a white and red striped blanket was in a corner of the room. A sink with a long handled pump and a towel invited him to clean up a bit. He figured out the pump and felt better after splashing his face with the cold water. He wiped the blood from his hairy body.

He glanced in a cracked mirror over the sink. He was not a pretty creature. He sighed. Bigfoot girl Lally liked him just the same.

He lay on the cot and slept again.

The sun lay long through the dusty window when he woke to the crunching of dry grass outside the door. Something stopped at the door.

He held his breath.

He checked his chronometer and gripped the sharp tool in his fist.

The door creaked open.

Zorster's toes. Errl farted and raised the metal tool.

The door opened all the way.

"What the blinkin' heck?"

Errl's answer came out sounding like a growl. The man in the checked shirt held a gun, like the metal thing the leader of the boys' pack had pointed at him yesterday.

Was it yesterday? So much. I came here to study and learn, to fade away without being seen, to leave with my friends and Dr. Teach after some fun and research on this new planet with the bright single sun, so strange, not to talk to the Humans, not to be seen. Now the tables are upside down for poor Errl.

"What and who in Sam Hill are *you?*" The man took in Errl's scotched face, the bloody towel, his ragged fur and bleeding feet. The man put down the gun. He took a step forward.

Errl put down the sharp tool and screamed.

"I'm not going to hurt you, son."

Brushing past the man, he rushed out the door.

"Stop! I want to help you!"

He ran like all the devils of Zorster were after him. Twigs snapped beneath his feet and branches whipped his face.

The chronometer read six hours and it was the second day.

He knew he was too sore and bruised to run far. Far away he heard dogs and men. Behind him the trapper's voice called out.

"Come back! You've nothing to fear from me, boy. Come back, you don't know what you're doing."

Where should I run? I can't keep this up.

The shrubs and fir began to thin as he loped at an angle through the forest. Ahead there were houses, possible shelter and help.

He had reached the town.

Chapter Eight

Houses that looked like boxes spread across the valley. Errl crouched in the tall grass on the edge of town. A mist hung over the town as the sun went down.

I'm cold and hungry again. I don't like this place. It's too quiet. I smell humans and the four legged animals that howl and chase me. Is there another door open anywhere? Another can of food? I might take a chance. I can hide. I see openings underground and steps. I can hide. I can hide.

He shivered. Behind him he heard the voice of the trapper with the gun.

He didn't fire his weapon. Why not?

The trapper wasn't like the leader of the children's pack. He didn't shout at Errl and he didn't shoot at him. The Bigfoot boy thought hard.

Maybe the man is my friend.

Twigs crunched behind him and he whirled around. The man in the checked shirt stood there. He was half hidden by the trees. He had the long gun in his hand but he didn't raise it. His voice was low and kind. Errl growled.

"Take it easy, my hairy friend. Not the first time I seen a Sasquatch."

Sasquatch? The word was familiar. Errl wished he'd read his history of Earth in class. Was that the human's name for Errl?

"Sasquatch." He formed the strange sounds with his thick tongue. The man bared his teeth in what was recognized was a smile, and Errl smiled back.

"That's it, pal. You're a smart one. Bigfoot and Sasquatch are the same. My name's Joe Locke."

Errl stood up to his full height, just under seven feet tall. The man backed up.

"Whoa, buddy. You're a big 'un, you are."

The man knows my Earth name. There are others of us here? I've heard stories. Where? Where are my Kinfolk on Earth? I must find them. They will help me find my ship.

"Where you come from, big buddy?"

Errl bared his teeth. He tried to speak. He copied what the man said.

Why didn't I pay attention when Teach taught us Earth words? Earth words are different in different places, but I know this place is called Kootenays *and this is* Canada *and I'm a* Sasquatch *or* Bigfoot.

He tried to remember his lessons. Teach tried to prepare his class. Every year a new class, every year a new lesson and a new location.

This was a favorite location, close to water and shelter, far from cities, hidden by mountains, rich in nature.

Close to my Kinfolk here on Earth? Dr. Teach didn't tell me that. What does this human know about us? Why doesn't he shoot at me? Why is he different?

The trapper seemed to read his thoughts.

"Yes, I've seen others like you. Deep in the woods, high on the mountains. They let me be and I let them be. But you're the first I seen that's come down from the mountains, so close to town, and you look like a young 'un, I'd say, no more than just into your teens."

He seems kind. I need food. I need shelter and I need to meet my ship in eight Earth days. I'm scared and cold and hungry. Where is Mam? Where is Teach and my sister and Berndt? Why did they go away and leave me, anyhow, and what happened to our ship? So many questions. I wish I'd listened more in class. I wish I'd stayed with my friends.

"Down. Get down. I hear the dogs and the posse."

He knew what the trapper said because he heard the same thing. From the middle of town came the baying of dogs and the thunder of engines starting. He knew they were looking for him.

The tall grass hid the Bigfoot boy as he ducked into it again, at the edge of town.

"Come with me, boy." The trapper bent over and waved his arm when he thought it was safe to go ahead. "I got a son at home, too. He'll be looking for me now. Let's go real slow and real quiet. My son always wanted a pet. Maybe you'll do." He grinned at his own joke.

Errl understood. He crept through the weeds and grass behind the trapper. The trapper led him to a low building with a porch. A yellow square of light showed him that someone else was in the building.

Danger.

He lay flat on the ground. His chronometer cut into his wrist. It was eight chronos. Late. A single moon was rising over the town. He could no longer hear the men and dogs. A boy like him stood in the square of yellow light in the trapper's house. The trapper was at the door, waving to him and hissing. He bared his teeth and got up.

I have to trust him. If I don't trust him the men with guns will be happy. They'll find me and kill me or put me in a cell.

He ran to the door and joined the man and the boy. The boy stood near his shoulder.

"Dad! You got a Bigfoot!" The boy bared his teeth in what Errl recognized was a universal smile.

Errl smiled back and growled. The man clapped the boy on his back.

"You bet, Joey. I got a Bigfoot. I found him in our cabin in the woods out back. I followed him. He came this way."

That name again. That's me or somebody like me. Are there others? What do this man and the little human know about Bigfoot? My Teach said they call us Bigfoot or Sasquatch. I remember now. I wish I'd paid more attention in school. Teach, where are you now? Where is my Pa and Mam? Do they miss me already? Do they know I'm lost?

The man appeared to read his thoughts again.

"He's lost and hurt. I took him home."

"They're hunting him, Dad. Pack leader Pete Puffin and his buddies got their guns out and their ATVs and dogs. They're looking for this guy. He scared the heck out of the Cubs in the trees out back of the Oldboy River."

"Yeah, I know, Joey. They're a scared yellow bunch. We've got to help our friend here. Let's hide him. But first I think he needs food."

"Sure, Dad. What do Bigfoot eat?"

"I don't know. This one ate a can of beans at the cabin."

"Beans?"

Errl burped. He smiled again and sat down. The chair broke.

"Easy, boy. Don't break our furniture. You're a big 'un, you are."

"Dad, the whole town's full of the news. He was on the six o'clock news and everything. We got reporters here from far away as Toronto, and a woman from Laval University in Quebec, and a couple of biologists from Vancouver."

"We'll never get away with it. We can only hide him so far," the trapper said. "But let's give him some cheese pizza and try to hide him in the basement in the spare room. They'll look for him there if they come here. But they won't suspect we've got him. I hope."

"I wish we had a dog. I told you a dog would protect me when you're gone. A dog would be company for me, Dad. If we had a dog he could protect Bigfoot."

"Joey, I know you want a pet. The answer is no. Some day maybe, when we have time to train a pet. Too many dogs in Parsnip Creek. I don't like them. Cats neither."

"What about your cabin, Dad? Do they know the Bigfoot went there?"

"I don't know, son. We've got to try. The poor beast's hurt and hungry, and looks like he's far from home. I don't know if Bigfoot eat meat. Let's try Pizza Pan cheese pizza cold because I'm home late, and maybe he'd like a cola."

Errl sat on the floor and ate pizza. He finished the whole pizza and looked around for B-E-A-N-S. Joe the trapper gave him a jug of cold water and he drank the jug down, water slopping over his hairy jaws. He wiped his face and gave the jug back. He farted. Joe gave him a cola and Errl snorted and woofed with appreciation.

"Dad, he really smells bad."

"I know. Bigfoot don't bathe like we do. I think he's been in the river, though. He was wet when I saw him, just drying out on my cot under the Bay blanket."

Errl spent the night in their basement.

Chapter Nine

Errl seemed doomed not to sleep well on this planet. He woke up two or three hours later. The house was dark. A bit of light spilled through a small window in the basement. He hunched under the quilt the trapper gave him. He was cold. He could hear engines running up and down the street outside and men's voices were loud, likely hunting him.

Will they find me here? Where is the kind man and his son? I'm alone in this big dark room. I hear noises in the night. They think I'm dangerous. Am I safe?

He was not safe. He knew he was not safe. He felt the chronometer on his wrist in the dark. His eyes were quite good in the dark. It was long past six chronos. The rescue airpod had come and gone without him. He set the chronometer to count the Earth days. Eight more days. This was the second day. Ten more loops of the moon around the Earth, his Teach had said. That was what the Humans called ten days, and it was a long time to be alone. Lost on Earth.

Thud. Thud. Thud.

What's that?

Someone was coming downstairs.

A light flicked on. He held his breath, his heart thumping and a snake of fear coursed through him. He released his breath and laughed when he saw who it was.

His laughter sounded like rocks crashing together in a sack. Joey stood at the bottom of the steps, a little flashlight in one hand.

"Are you all right, Bigfoot?" Joey asked. "Can I turn on the light down here?"

He grunted. He began to sense what Joey was saying. He began to know the strange words. He remembered the English classes in MiddleSchool, and what Teach had tried to tell him.

"Yes," he said, but knew that to Joey, it sounded like a growl. The boy came forward.

"I won't hurt you," he said.

Grunting again, he threw the quilt off the cot. The cot sagged beneath his weight, his legs hanging over the end.

"You're not comfortable on that bed," Joey said. "Let's find you something better, pal."

Again the Bigfoot simply grunted, then rubbed his eyes.

"You're hurt. You're dirty and bruised. I'll help you."

Errl held out his hands. Joey came closer.

"I'll get a pail of hot water and wash you," the boy said. "You look ill. There's a sink down here. Just a minute, dude."

He stood still as the boy washed the dried blood and mud from his fur. He let the boy wash his hands and feet.

"We should have done this last night," Joey said. "We were all tired."

"Tired," he said. He knew that word.

"What did you say, dude?"

Tired.

"I thought you spoke English for a minute. Well, never mind. I'm just hearing things. It's late."

Engines roared past the window. A man's voice shouted.

"They're pretty close." Joey wrung out the cloth, rummaging around in the chest beside the cot.

"Here it is. Some antibiotic ointment. It'll make those wounds feel better, pal."

Thank you.

"Are you hungry?"

No response.

"Guess I heard wrong when I thought you talked. You just grunt. Nobody upstairs, right?"

Nobody upstairs?

"Except my dad." Joey laughed. "That's not what I meant. Empty, right?" He whirled his finger at his head. "I'm just whistling Dixie here with you, pal."

"Whistling Dixie with you, pal." The effort cost Errl a great deal. His jaw and tongue were not made to talk Earth languages. Not even with Teach's help. He tried to remember. He wished he had paid more attention in class.

"Yes," he said. "Someone upstairs."

"I'll be a monkey's uncle." Joey whistled. "You surprise the heck out of me, dude. Just when I think you're not the sharpest knife in the drawer. You surprise me, big monkey."

Monkey?

An image of a chattering creature, cousin to this Human. Errl bared his teeth in a smile, made chittering noises and jumped up and down. He scratched his sides. He made a noise like rocks in a sack. Joey grinned.

"Dad, come see this!"

They knew he was a smart cookie after that. He was proud.

Their neighbor next door peered into the lighted square of glass. He put down his binoculars.

"Maude, come see this."

"Lordy, Clyde. What have they got in their basement?"

"Looks a lot like that Bigfoot that Pete's been looking for all day."

"Get on the horn in the morning. Pete'll be happy to see this."

"Why not tonight?"

"Go to bed. This ain't the time to call nobody."

"What do you mean, Maude? Pete'll want to know."

"Pete's out there on his ATV with his buddies, looking for the Bigfoot. You got his cell number?"

"Well, no."

"All right then."

"I'll call their land line at the house."

Pete's wife answered. She slammed down the phone when she heard what her neighbors had to say. That crazy Peter Puffin, if he'd been home he'd of nabbed that big monkey right away. She dialed a number. Peter had turned off his cell phone.

Oh, well, he'd be over to Joe Locke's in the morning. That monkey wasn't going nowhere.

She went back to bed.

Back at the trapper's house, Joey made a bed on the floor and tucked his new friend in for the night. Errl grunted.

"My name Errl," he said, pointing to himself.

"Errl? That's your name? Mine's Joey, but then you know that, don't you?"

Errl's shaggy head nodded up and down and he closed his eyes. He felt safe there.

Pete came home at dawn. His wife met him at the door.

"I know where that space critter is right now, Pete," she said. "I got a call from Clyde Barrister last night. He's over to Joe the trapper's place, in their basement."

"Who is?" Pete asked.

"Why, the big monkey. He's there right now. Clyde done saw him there, in their basement, plain as daylight."

"Get the guys on the horn." Pete rubbed his eyes and grinned. He grabbed his gun. "We got work to do."

"I'll call the sheriff, too."

"You do that, Mrs. Puffin. We're on our way."

Chapter Ten

The next morning Peter Puffin found Errl backed up against a wall in Joe Locke's basement, huddled under a Spiderman quilt. The trapper and his son couldn't save the Bigfoot boy. Peter Puffin thought very highly of himself and liked to take charge.

"You're coming with us." Puffin brandished a very long gun. Other men crowded behind him. They stared at Errl. One of the men wore a shiny sheriff's badge. He held a taser. A woman pushed forward. Someone screamed.

"Leave him alone." Joey Locke, the trapper's eleven-year-old son, pulled at the Cub leader's sleeve. "He never hurt anybody. Let him go back to the forest."

"He don't live in the forest, Joey," Puffin said. "He come from some kind of spaceship out near Oldboy River. We seen it, the kids and I. Sittin' in the sky one minute. The next it come flaming to the ground. We watched it fall. Next thing you know this Sasquatch shows up."

"Yeah, Pete says he's some kind of alien."

"We got to get in touch with the RCMP detachment out Cranbrook way."

"We got to take this beastie with us," the sheriff said. "We'll hold him for a while in a jail cell, see how he likes that."

"Handcuff him, Jeff." Puffin backed away, still waving his shotgun in Errl's direction.

"I don't think you have to do that," Joe Locke said. "He's harmless, I'll vouch for him."

"You're under suspicion, too, Joe," the sheriff said. "Keeping a known criminal under wraps."

Errl raised his arms. He tried to speak. All the men heard were grunts and growls.

"Look, he's wearing something on his arm."

"Must be a weapon."

"Give it here." The sheriff snapped large handcuffs on Errl's wrists. He tried to remove the chronometer. Errl whirled around and growled.

"Oh, testy, ain't he?"

"Yeah, must be a weapon."

"It looks like a watch," Joey Locke cried. "It might be something he needs to get back to his friends. Like a GPS or something."

"More like a ray gun, most likely." Puffin stood back. "I'm not getting close enough to this beast to find out, though. He almost killed us in the woods near Oldboy River."

"He did not!" Joey was close to tears. "He wouldn't hurt nobody."

"Joe, your boy's calling me a liar. What are you gonna do about it?"

The sheriff was talking on his Blackberry. "RCMP on their way here. They'll be a few more minutes. We need the paddy wagon and a lot of extra guys with tranks to take this thing in."

"He's not a thing. He's our friend."

"Careful, son," the trapper said. "We got to go slow here. This is out of our hands now."

"Well, we can try, Dad."

"Your dad and you kept a dangerous alien in your home overnight. You're lucky you're still alive."

"That's not true."

"Joey, if your mom were here this never would have happened." Mrs. Puffin put her arm around Joey's shoulders. "May she rest in peace."

"Don't you talk about my mom," Joey cried. "She would have liked him, too."

What's happening? Errl wondered. They put my hands in these metal things. I can't move my arms. They tried to take my chronometer. I'll never get back to my ship if they do. This is the worst thing that's ever happened to me.

He looked at the trapper and his son. *I thought you were my friends.*

"I'm sorry, Bigfoot," Joe Locke said. "I'm sorry, pal. We really tried to keep this from happening. We tried to keep you safe."

Joey shrugged off Mrs. Puffin's hand on his shoulder. He ran upstairs.

"There's lots of Sasquatch around here. Everybody knows that. They leave us alone. This isn't the first one." Joey's father looked unhappy.

"This is the first alien we know of, Joe."

"You don't know that."

"He tried to kill the boys and me out near the River. We saw his spaceship go down."

"He'll want to rejoin his friends."

"Didn't seem too keen on that the other night. Walked right into camp."

The RCMP arrived with dogs. Errl shuddered and put his handcuffed wrists over his eyes. They gave him a shot to sedate him and then led him quietly up the stairs and into the paddy wagon.

Upstairs, Joey and his father watched them drive away.

"Guess they think they're heroes," the trapper said.

"They're taking him down to the jail house, aren't they?" Joey asked.

"Yes. For now."

"Then what?"

"That depends. Maybe in a truck to Vancouver where they can study him at the University there."

"Dad?"

"Yeah, I know, son."

"We got to do something. What they're doing is really ill."

"I know."

"This is a really awesome dude. He might be from outer space. He came to us for help."

"I know what you're saying, Joey."

"We gotta help him, Dad."

"Yes."

"First thing in the morning I'm going down to the jail and bring him some food. What do you think he'd like?"

"I don't think they like meat."

The sheriff turned around from locking the paddy wagon. "Joe, if it weren't for your boy here, you'd be coming with us," he said. "Well, gotta go now. And Joey?"

"Yeah, Sheriff Jeff?"

"You come on down to the jail tomorrow. You bring that Bigfoot some grub. I don't mind at all. Reporters will be here soon. Got to go. See you tomorrow, young Joe."

"I'll be there, sheriff."

Errl hunched in his cell on a hard cot with one blanket. *I still have my chronometer. They couldn't figure out the lock. Thanks, Pa. Thanks, Teach.*

The strange young Human was a puzzle. He thought the human boy might be a friend. He put his handcuffed hands in front of him, then rolled under the blanket. In the distance, the phones started to ring.

It was the third day.

Chapter Eleven

Nanoseconds whirled on Errl's chronometer. He was in jail and the Sheriff had left for an hour. Deputy Carl was in charge. Carl hunched in front of the Dell computer playing Microsoft Halo 2 Vista. Errl stared at him through the bars.

"What are you looking at, creep?" A shiver snaked down Carl's spine.

Have to get out. Have to meet ship.

"Okay, what have you got to say?"

Let me out. Let me out.

"All I hear is a lot of grunting and bleeping from you, creep. Now be quiet and let me play the game. Sheriff fed you. You got water. Leave me alone."

He rattled the bars.

"I *told* you. I'm not going to tell you a second time. I'm warning you, dude." Carl took out his taser. Just then the door opened and Joey stuck his head in.

"What do you want, kid?"

"Sheriff said I could visit the Bigfoot any time. I come to bring him lunch."

"He had lunch."

"He doesn't like jail food."

"How do you know, kid? Now go away and leave me alone. I'm busy. Sheriff won't be back for another hour. Come back then. Better yet, go home and don't come back at all."

"Sheriff said I could visit."

"Go home, kid."

Carl pushed Joey toward the door. Errl watched. Carl closed the door and he could see Joey standing at the window outside on the street. He howled and banged on the bars, grasping them in both hands and pulled. They bent like soft butter in his hairy paws.

"Hey! Cut that out."

Taser in hand, Carl jabbed it through the bars, catching Errl on the belly where the hair was thin. Errl roared, grabbed the end of the taser, pulling Carl toward him. The man was swearing, wrestling to get the taser back, but finally let go. Errl swung the taser, catching Carl on the side of the neck. The man screamed and went down. The bars of the cell bulged outward as keys skidded across the floor just as the sheriff walked in.

"What the bloomin' brown sugar, Carl, you twit?"

Errl stopped roaring and sat down on his cot. Joey peeked in through the door.

"Sheriff, I saw it all. Carl tried to taser him for no reason. And he wouldn't let me visit my friend."

"That right, Carl?" The sheriff pushed a foot against Carl's writhing body. "Are you all right?"

"No, Jeff. Dang beast tried to kill me. I'm going to write up a report as soon as I can get to my feet. Used my own taser against me."

"I'd say you had it coming, Deputy Dawg." The sheriff unsnapped the large handcuffs on his belt and entered the cell. "Here, Bigfoot, I have to do this."

He chained Errl to the cot, then satisfied, stood up with a grunt and locked the doors again. "Looks like he did some damage here all right, Joey. Can't have this. Can't have him attacking my deputy, no matter how stoopid the deputy might be."

"No, sheriff. It won't happen again." Joey put his hands on the bars and stared at Errl. "You hear that? No more violence. No matter what they do to you, pal."

"No more." Errl huddled on the narrow cot in chains.

"Here, guess there's no real need of these," the sheriff said, reconsidering his actions. He removed the handcuffs and chains. "You behave yourself now, boy, or I'll have to put them back on. Though I got a pure suspicion you could break these chains in half, eat them and spit out the pieces if you wanted to, big guy."

"He wouldn't do that, sheriff," Joey said.

Carl was still moaning on the floor.

"Get up, you twit." Sheriff Jeff thumped down a wad of memo paper. "Make a report. You can do that much, can't you? And remember in the future how that taser feels."

Carl moaned again. "I sure won't forget this, young Locke."

Joey smiled. "I sure hope you won't, Deputy Carl. Why don't you run on home now to your mommy?"

"You little SOB."

"Hey, what are you calling my young friend here?" Sheriff Jeff looked up from his paperwork. "Get up, Carl, dang it, and go home, you useless catfish."

"Bigfoot lover," Carl muttered in Joey's direction. Joey slid a peanut butter sandwich under the bars toward Errl, who grabbed it and began to eat. He cradled a large greasy paper bag in his other arm.

Pizza, Errl thought. *And something else.* He finished the sandwich and gulped some flavored water. They were spoiling him today.

"Yes I am. He's my buddy."

"You don't have any buddies at school, do you?" Carl sat up and held his head. "Holy nutcrackers, that hurts. I feel like I got hit by a tank."

"I got my good friends," Joey said.

Errl hung his head. Joey was too good for this world.

Chapter Twelve

"They trashed our house," Joey said. He sat hunched in front of Errl. An empty Chow Mein box and a spoon sat next to Errl on his cot. Crusts littered the floor. "At least they took off those handcuffs." Joey leaned forward and frowned.

"They threw a note through the window on a rock. *Alien lover leave town.* I know who it was. Peter Puffin and his guys. Or somebody from my school. They're giving me a bad time. I don't know how much longer I can keep coming here to see you. Maybe this is my last visit."

Errl bared his teeth and tried to smile. He rubbed his wrists. He sometimes understood the boy now. Errl remembered part of his language lessons but it was too late, maybe. Joey's hair was blue, like his sister Torannee's hair. Errl's heart ached for home.

Two exobiologists stood in the hallway, anxious to poke and prod the Sasquatch. Reporters again clamored outside the small town jail. A photographer unlawfully peered through the bars. Joey heard the whir of a video camera.

"It's like being in a circus," Joey said.

Errl pulled on the hair by his ears. His body was matted with dried blood, his hair thin in some places, although he had been cleaned up somewhat the night before in Joe Locke's basement. The treatment he received at the jail had opened his wounds anew.

"You're ugly." Joey smiled. "You need to visit a spa."

Errl bared his teeth and grunted.

"Trash your house?" he asked. His English was improving. The effort it cost him was huge. His throat and jaws weren't formed right to speak Earth languages.

"Yeah." Joey rubbed his face with a dirty hand. "We don't know who it was. Pete or who. The kids might have done it."

"Kids?" *The camp, the Cub scout leader, the dogs, the guns...*

"Not the Cubs." Joey seemed to read his mind. "The kids in my class. They say I'm a Bigfoot lover. They say if my mom was alive I'd be different. They call me names. Dirty alien Sasquatch creep."

"They bully Joey?"

"Where'd you hear that, pal? Yeah, they're bullies. Some of the teachers back them up. Not my teacher. She's neat. My dad understands. And you."

"Joey's my pal?"

"Yeah, buddy. But I don't know for how long. I might not come back. It's not safe." Joey looked away.

"Last visit? Errl is sad."

"I can't take it, pal. This morning somebody trashed our house. My dad was at the cabin. What's going to happen next?"

"Joey not my friend? Errl needs a gummy wad."

"I don't have any gum this morning, Errl. I'm sorry."

"Not gum. Gummy wad. Errl is hungry."

"You just ate a box of chow mein and another cheese pizza. Holy crow, how much can you eat?"

"Errl needs a gummy wad."

"Oh, I see. You chew your cud."

"Yes."

"Like a cow. Like a darn cow. Well, Sheriff says you're out of here today. Going to a big city, pal. I'm outa here, too, Errl. I can't take it anymore. You're on your way in a paddy wagon to UBC in Vancouver. I'm going back to school. I don't like it. But I have to go to school. I have to try and fit in. This is goodbye."

"Goodbye, Joey."

"That's all? Just 'goodbye, Joey'?"

"Yes." Errl sighed. "Errl very sad. Have to meet friends in…" He checked his chronometer."Five days. Been here five days, five more days. Going to big city far away. They'll cut me up in pieces and put pieces in chemicals. Never see home again."

"Not my problem, dude."

"No, Joey. Not your problem."

"Do you have to be so darn *pleasant*?"

"Errl not a nice Bigfoot. Errl made trouble for Joey and Pa."

"Yeah, you did, pal. You made big trouble. Big time."

"Sorry, pal." It sounded like a growl. Joey scratched his head. He rubbed the side of his mouth with a grubby hand.

"This is goodbye. Do you have anything more to say, buddy?"

"Goodbye."

Joey left.

Errl stirred the remaining noodles in the chow mein box with a hairy hand. He sighed. *No more food. Have to eat jail slop. I don't like to admit this, Teach, but if you were here, you'd have to give up on me. I forgot where I left the airship. I know, should carry tech compass at all times on alien planet, you told us that. Over and over you told us that. I forgot, Teach. I left tech compass behind in my room on the small airpod. Good thing chronometer is locked on my arm. Good thing my head is attached to my neck.*

Goodbye, Dr. Teach. Goodbye Lally, Berndt, and Torannee. I don't think I'll see you again.

Chapter Thirteen

"Hello? Sheriff Jeff Ridge speaking."

"How are you, sheriff? I'm a reporter from the Milwaukee *Clarion*. We got something strange on the ticker this morning. Something about a Sasquatch captured in your town? Is that right?"

"Well, Mr. Reporter, you're only about the 220th pencil pusher to call tonight. I been so busy answering phones I don't have time for my prisoner."

"Prisoner? Would that be the Bigfoot, sheriff?"

"Just a minute." Three other phones were ringing off the desk. The sheriff punched call waiting on the call from the *Clarion*, call waiting twice more and put everyone on hold. Then he hung up.

"Sheriff?" It was his deputy, Carl, a useless boy who lived with his very rich and influential parents in their basement suite and worked only when it suited him. The useless twit was paid full wages. Sheriff Jeff sighed as two phones rang at the same time. He lifted each one then hung up. The deputy ambled to the single cell where Errl lay under the spare blanket.

"Sure is *big*, ain't he, Jeff?"

"Sure is." The sheriff stuffed a cigar in his mouth and lit it. The deputy coughed. All three phones rang.

"InterGlobal TV van's out front."

"Oh, darn."

"Want me to lock the door, Sheriff Jeff?" The deputy stared at Errl. Errl stared back.

"No, don't bother. They're here."

"It's past time for supper, ain't it?" Carl asked. "What's he eat?"

"Danged if I know." The sheriff blocked the door as a photographer with all his gear tried to get in. Behind him reporters and neighbors shouted and pushed at the windows and doorway. Rough hands pushed him back into his office. As he staggered backward, he drew his taser.

"That's enough. Anybody come one step farther and you get burnt."

"Watch out, sheriff. We're your neighbors. You don't want to hurt us. We just want a look at that there Bigfoot."

"Yes, what you got in there?"

The reporters were the worst. They wouldn't go back and they wouldn't give up. The deputy drew his pistol. His neighbors, grumbling and muttering about re-election, finally left.

"Put that down, Carl. Don't be a fool. Somebody might get hurt."

"Sheriff, with all respect..."

"You don't have a brain in your head, deputy. Put that gun away before you shoot yourself in the foot." Sheriff Jeff pushed a broad shoulder to the door against the reporters, stuck the taser through the crack in the door and blasted the photographer. He finally got the door closed and locked and leaned against the thick wood, panting. Carl drew circles in the air with his pistol.

"I'll protect you, sheriff."

"You'll do no such thing, Deputy Dawg. I told you to put that dang thing away and I meant it. Do as I say. Now let's check on our prisoner. I hope he ain't too scared."

Errl huddled on his cot in the cell and picked at the plate of food the sheriff had left him. There were mashed potatoes and peas and gravy, a dinner roll and Jello. It was all good. The sheriff was a good man.

I'm not scared.

"How you doing, big fella?" Sheriff Jeff peered through the bars. His charge was eating. He didn't look afraid. He didn't look like anything. The creature had no expression.

"He look scared, Jeff?" Carl slid his pistol back in the holster and patted the bulge under his lapels.

"Naw, he's not scared."

"Good. But maybe he should be."

"What do you mean by that, Carl?"

"You know, Jeff. Tomorrow the boys from the town hall are gonna get to him. Maybe lynch him. Maybe take him to Vancouver for *r-r-r-research*." The deputy grinned.

"Over my dead body."

"They can arrange that."

"You're enjoying this, aren't you?"

"Why, sheriff, of *course* not." Carl grinned again. He patted the gun under his coat lapels. "But it's the most excitement this town has had since the pigs ate granny."

"Deputy, I won't have any of that talk. We run a tight ship here in this town. Folks are reasonable."

"Sure they are, sheriff. That's why Pete Puffin and his good ol' boys run the spit out of Bigfoot here yesterday. With guns and everything."

"They had a story to tell."

"With emphasis on *story*. You buy into that alien spaceship story Pete is telling?"

"Well, no."

"Neither do I. Neither does anybody else. Pete's been into the cherry whiskey again."

"Now Carl."

"Well, what do you think, Jeff? Story like that."

Errl looked at the rounded plastic utensil the sheriff had left him. Maybe he should have eaten his supper with that? He licked his webbed fingers and wiped his mouth with a hairy arm. Mmmm good. He began to chew his cud.

"Critter looks tame enough." The deputy peered into the cell again. He leaned against the metal doors. "He ate the food you left him."

"Sure enough. Critter was hungry."

More, thought Errl. He pushed the plate toward Carl.

"I'll be switched if he don't want more."

"Seems to be smart." The sheriff pinched his lower lip. "Don't know for sure I want to hand him over to the RCMP tomorrow morning."

"You're gonna have to, aren't you?"

"Yeah. I'm gonna have to hand him over to the big cops."

"For secret *experiments*." Carl grinned.

"Cut that out, Carl. They're law and order around here."

"I thought that's what we were."

"That, too. But we don't have the manpower or cells strong enough for our hairy friend here. They'll take good care of him in Vancouver."

"Vancouver." Carl snorted.

"Vancouver," Errl said. It pained him to mouth the English words that Teach had taught his class before the trip.

"What? What did he say?"

"Settle down, Carl. He was just whistling and snorting like critters do."

"No, Jeff. He said *Vancouver*. Clear as daybreak."

"Carl, you've been working too hard. Go home now and get yourself a nice chicken dinner. Have a soda pop. Watch some TV and go to bed. I'll see you in the morning. First thing, mind you. The city cops will be here then. They want to do the paperwork early then leave around dawn."

They're planning something. I can almost understand their language. A little more thought... Vancouver. Is Vancouver my new friend?

Carl took his baton and rang it against all the bars in the cell. It clanged like a dozen bells. Errl flinched and held his huge hands against his ears. Carl laughed, turned and walked out of the office.

Chapter Fourteen

The police truck with the barred windows and rear heating left at dawn the next day. It was the sixth day.

Inside the back of the truck there were five RCMP guards, Errl, and a dog. The sedative they'd given Errl began to work and he sat on a bench in chains. He was very sleepy but sleep was not possible. The bench was hard, and the way they had him chained made sitting uncomfortable. The road across the mountains was rough. The guards drank coffee and ate muffins, and gave Errl a breakfast sandwich with ham, egg and cheese, but he couldn't eat it.

Behind the armored truck was a trailer with three RCMP horses and their groom.

"Hey, creep, go on and eat." One of the guards nudged Errl with his baton. "We want you alive when we get to Vancouver. The University boys there have work to do. They need you healthy."

"Leave him alone, Herman," another guard said. "He's not hurting anybody."

"He isn't helping anybody, either."

"Leave him alone."

"Now you sound like that trapper dude. Or the soft-hearted sheriff. We had to leave Cranbrook and Nelson short staffed on account of this alien creep. You hear that, Bigfoot?"

That word again. Bigfoot or Sasquatch, that was him. There were others?

The truck rumbled and roared up the steep Skyview and across the other side of the mountain to the ferry. Once across the deep green Goose Lake, the engine strained around the corkscrew bends of the treacherous Horseshoe Pass and then down to the valley below. Sleep finally overtook the Sasquatch boy in the back of the police vehicle as they rumbled across the valley and up the other side.

It was there the truck broke down.

Plumes of steam boiled from under the hood. The driver swore and stepped on the brakes. The guards in the back of the truck rapped on the window that separated them from the cab.

"What's going on?"

Errl snapped awake.

"We got to take the Bigfoot out of here. Truck might catch fire any minute."

"Well, let's unlock him. He's well tranked. He won't be any trouble. Hasn't been any trouble so far."

"I wouldn't be so sure, Johnny."

"Give us a break, Herman."

"Okay, then. It's on your head."

"Draw your gun."

"That's not necessary. Let's go, Bigfoot."

Errl stumbled to his feet, his chains left behind on the bench. He felt fine as he stepped from the truck, the cold air invigorating. Inside the truck it had been too hot. Bigfoot were made for cold. Their home planet was much cooler than Earth. Their body fur protected them unless they were sick or weakened in some way, as Errl had been after he fell into the river and escaped from the Cub leader and his friends. Before he had met the trapper.

Before I lost hope.

He lumbered into the bright sunlight of late afternoon.

"We were making good time, too."

"We've been lucky so far," Herman said.

"Too good to last." The guards stretched their legs. It had been a couple of hours since the last break.

The groom stepped out of the trailer behind the steaming armored vehicle.

"Should I take the horses out?"

"Maybe let them out for a bit to graze beside the road. We'll just have to limp into the next town if we can find a ride, and find a service station open."

"Pretty late to get a mechanic this time of day in a small town," the other guard said.

"Yeah."

The groom led the horses out on the side of the road. Errl, sedated, sat on the trailer hitch. He scratched under his arms. The first horse, a bay gelding sixteen hands high, spooked when he saw Errl and tore the rope from the groom's hands. The other two ran away as well, snorting and bucking. Errl stood up to his full nearly seven feet. Three guards drew their pistols.

"Easy now," one said. The dog growled and the officer from the K-9 corps held tightly to the dog's collar. The groom ran after the horses, but came back with only one. He swore at Errl, but took care to avoid the huge hairy creature and led the horse behind the trailer. He turned and hurried off to try and locate the other two.

I won't hurt you, wonderful creature, Errl tried to send his thoughts to the animal. The horse pawed the frozen ground and made a sound like the exhaust of a supercharged Chevy 383 engine. Trucks and cars roared by; their occupants stared but didn't stop.

"All right then. Sit down, dude, and you won't get hurt." One of the Mounties snapped extra large handcuffs onto Errl's hands and pointed to the pavement. Errl sat on the hard surface of the road.

I can break these easy when the humans least expect it.

The groom returned with the two horses. They pranced on delicate feet around Errl, who thought gentle thoughts at them.

Hairy creature talks to horse, horse thinks he's kind.

Thank you, horse.

A minivan wove down the highway, slowing when the teenaged driver saw Errl and the horses, and the RCMP truck at the side of the road. The other teens hooted and waved bottles in the air.

The van veered to the side of the road, making contact with a horse. Although it didn't go down, it let out a painful whinny.

Are you all right? The Mounties waved the teens out of their vehicle. "Is he all right?"

The groom surveyed his charge. "Seems to be. No thanks to Mr. Demolition here."

The teens spilled out of their van, throwing empty bottles into the ditch.

"Too late, kids," the Mounties said. "You're under arrest."

"And what are you gonna do with us? Your truck is smoking and your horses are all over the road. You've got a big monkey sitting on your tailgate and at least half a dozen cops on foot. Kiss my apples."

"Let's see your ID, sir. You're all underage and you're getting a ticket for driving under the influence, reckless driving, resisting arrest, and anything else I can think of."

"Just because your freaking horse ran into my van?"

"Sir, you ran into the animal. You're endangering yourself and others. Now come with me."

"No, I can't leave the van here. My dad would kill me. It's his van."

"Someone sober may drive home, sir."

"All right, who's sober back there?"

There were several answers. The horse made a sound like the wind on vinyl siding and the teens drove away, veering all over the road.

"We'll get you, punks," Herman shouted.

Errl watched.

"We'll be back," the young driver said. "See you in hell."

They didn't see the RCMP when they got back. They saw Errl.

Chapter Fifteen

"Can I help you boys?" The trucker backed his semi-trailer a few yards and leaned out of the open window.

Officer Herman wiped his forehead and took off his hat. "I think so. Bob, put the horses back. Todd and Johnny, keep an eye on our prisoner."

"My gosh, what's *that*?" The trucker got out of his cab. He stared at Errl.

"Our prisoner. We phoned ahead but it'll be another hour before reinforcements get here. Can you give us a ride to the next garage so we could get this truck towed and fixed?"

"Ee-yah, I'm not supposed to take riders. But you're Mounties, all of you except him, ain't you? Guess it would be okay."

"Just to the next town."

"Yeah, okay."

But something about the situation with the cops and their prisoner didn't sit right with the trucker.

Help. You look like a kind human, truck driver. Help me.

Errl pleaded with his eyes. The truck driver looked more closely at him.

"Say, he looks pretty sad, don't he? What you fellows been doing to him?"

"We're taking him to UBC for research and observation."

"That so?" The truck driver scratched his chin. "Looks like a big monkey to me. He smart?"

"Oh, no. Some kind of Bigfoot the sheriff found near Cranbrook."

"There's something about them eyes..." The truck driver peered at Errl. Errl gazed back and spoke.

"What the heck?"

"What did he say?"

Errl growled and spoke again. "I want to go home."

"Home? Where's that, son?" The truck driver patted one of the horses as the groom led it onto the side of the road. The truck driver was fond of animals. He didn't like to see an animal mistreated. Even a big monkey like the Bigfoot. He was a kind man like the trapper and Joey.

"Home." Errl gestured with a free hand to the sky.

"The stars?"

"Yes-s-s..." Errl grunted again. He looked up. It was the seventh day. His chronometer glinted in the sun.

"Say, he's got some kind of watch on. This dude's almost human. Where did you say you guys were taking him?"

The guards glanced at each other.

"Vancouver."

"Yeah. To the University for research? I don't think so."

Herman put his hand on his gun holster. He grinned.

"I think we will, fellow. You just go on your way now."

"Well, okay. I sure don't want to cause no trouble." The truck driver turned away. Then, as though he had forgotten something, he turned around again. He winked at Errl and made a motion with his hand. The guards were looking at Errl and didn't see the truck driver gesture. He got into his cab and started the engine. The engine rumbled and the truck backed up a few more feet. The guards stepped back.

"Hey, watch it, buddy."

"*Now, Bigfoot!*" The trucker threw open the door, hung out the cab on the running board, put a beefy hand out for Bigfoot, and pulled him into the cab. He floored the semi and the truck screamed away, gaining speed as it plowed along the shoulder of the road.

The guards fired at the truck but missed. They called for an all points bulletin on their cell phone with the license number of the truck. The steam hissed from the police vehicle as they waited helplessly with the groom, the driver, and the three police horses on the side of the deserted highway.

They were hundreds of miles from the nearest RCMP station.

The truck driver laughed and swerved off the road half a mile down the highway.

"We're going back, big boy," he said, and took a side road.

Errl grunted and bared his teeth.

"Thank you," he said. "I go home." He pointed to the sun. "Ship come take me home."

"Oh, you're going to meet a *space* ship? You ain't no regular Bigfoot then? No wonder they're so interested in you, big fellow."

"Errl alien."

"Yes. You're an alien. Holy smokes, that's awesome. Wait'll I tell my wife about this. Say, you ever drink Kokanee beer?" The truck driver grinned, gunning the motor around narrow country roads.

"They got a Bigfoot statue twelve, fourteen feet high, in their front yard. Just like you, pal. I'll take you to see it sometime. We'll have a party."

"Thank you," Errl said politely. He bared his teeth and settled back against the cloth seats. He was enjoying himself. This was just like the airship before it went down. The truck rocketed around another bend in the road. From far away they could hear sirens. The driver laughed.

Errl laughed, too, but he sounded like a forest of great apes knocking coconuts together. The driver roared again with the sheer joy of setting a fellow creature free, and Errl, though he didn't understand, put a huge paw on the trucker's shoulder and snorted.

"We're just like a couple of cowboys," shouted the trucker. "Yee haw. Don't worry about me, pal," the trucker continued. "I got three sets of plates and I drive in ten states and Mexico."

They followed the path of the Oldboy River to the spot Errl knew, close by the trapper's cabin. Here the trucker let him off. He hugged the driver, waved and disappeared into the forest.

He didn't see the van behind them on a logging road, driving in a cloud of dust up to the spot where Errl got off. The teens were very quiet now that their beer was gone. The young men were very curious about him. They set off on foot after him after the trucker had backed up and returned to town. He knew the teens were behind him but he didn't suspect they could travel as fast as they did. He thought he'd seen the last of them, after their van bumped the horse, who had whinnied like the wind on vinyl siding.

"Shhhh," The young driver grinned and wiped his mouth with a grubby hand. The other three trod behind in his footsteps. Errl hiked without a backward look into the forest. They didn't think he knew they followed him.

See you in hell. What did they mean by that? By Zorster's demons, maybe they had a faith. His Mam had a faith. She worshipped gods and taught Errl about Zorster, the main god in the religion of their part of Planet X. It was important to have a faith, said Mam. Pa and Errl weren't sure. But it made Mam happy. That's what counted.

Mam should be happy. Pa and Errl agreed on that.

Where was she now? Errl missed his Kinfolk.

Behind him, the young humans trudged to keep up. Errl slowed his pace. He was tired anyway and curious about the young men. They had helped him to get away, he thought. They might be friends, like Joey.

His Teach told Errl he was too trusting. What was wrong with that? One problem. *Who were the good Kinfolk on this strange new world? Was it Joey and his father? Joey, who had left him? The sheriff, who yelled at the cruel deputy? The RCMP, who kept the kind horses? Or could he trust nobody?* He looked behind and saw the teens trudging in his steps. He liked to play games and this was definitely a game. *We'll have a party,* he thought, and bared his teeth in that Bigfoot grin which scared the deputy.

Chapter Sixteen

"Hey, man, slow down," one of the teens called. He was tall and out of shape, the result of too much fast food, beer and sitting down to play video games rather than out on the soccer grounds like his three friends.

"He's just ahead of us through the bush, stompin' and ambling along. Not a care in his shaggy head. Say, do you think he's dangerous?"

"Nah, you saw the look in his eyes. He just wanted to get away from those cops. Say, I wonder if there's a reward on his hairy head? I bet there is."

"That's why we're following him, man."

"Stop, you handsome dude." The driver threw a rock in Errl's direction. He heard it thump a few feet past his head and turned, peering through the trees at the boys. Like Joey, they might be friends, but then again, they might not. He grunted. He had known all along they were behind him, and being curious he had let them walk this far, into the woods, into Bigfoot land.

"He's trying to talk to us."

"Do you think he heard us following him from the road?"

"He must have heard us. He thinks we're okay. Are we?"

"Sure, we are, dude."

"You okay?" Errl made an effort to speak English. The boys understood him.

"Yeah, we're okay, man." They began to run toward him and he backed up, not sure what they were doing. "Hey, don't be scared. We're your friends."

"Yeah, you got a cola?" They laughed. Errl bared his teeth and grinned. They stopped.

"Hey, that's not friendly."

"I think he's smiling."

"The cops after you, hairy dude?" The teens approached him. The bravest of them walked ahead, led by the driver who seemed to be a leader. The other three hung behind. "We're your friends. They're after us, too." They laughed.

Sounding like drums beating out of tune, he laughed along with them.

"Cops after Errl."

"That your name? Errl? Cool." One of the teens came within a few feet and offered a stick of gum. He took it. "Oh, a gummy wad."

"What's that, man? A gummy wad? Oh, yeah. Sure. A gummy wad." The teen laughed again.

He had found new friends, like Joey. He was happy as he chewed the wad of gum.

"You going back to the trapper's cabin, man?"

"Joe Locke?" Errl asked. His voice was hoarse and the boys caught only grunts and bleeps.

"What's that you say?"

"Not understand Errl?"

"No, not understand."

They surrounded the Bigfoot. One of the teens scuffed his foot in the frozen dirt near Errl's foot. "Say, what's wrong with your feet? They look sore."

"Errl's feet are sore."

"Any more like you in these woods?"

"Say, where are we, anyway? I think we should get back before we're lost." The boy swept a lock of hair from his eyes and played with the ring in his lip. "Your dad's gonna be so mad, Puffin."

"I got an idea that will make him happy," Pete's son said.

"You go?" Errl asked. He stroked the boy's head. Pete's son grinned.

"Yeah. We go."

Errl watched them jumping over fallen logs and crashing through the forest, much louder than when they had followed him. Errl's hearing was very good and he had let them find him. He was lonely, and these boys looked a lot like his friend Joey. But he didn't know they were not his friends.

Perhaps, though, later they would be?

Chapter Seventeen

A small lake sparkled under the late afternoon sun. Errl crept to its cold waters and drank. Under his hairy face he flushed when he glimpsed his reflection. A strong young male Bigfoot gazed back at him from the mirrored green surface. Was that him? The healing cream young Joey had applied to his wounds soothed his broken skin, and the blood and dried mud were washed from his body, leaving his hair thick and silky. He had lost weight and trimmed some body fat. His muscles rippled. Only the pads of his feet felt sore and bruised.

With a finger, he touched his face just as a fish broke the surface of the lake. Ripples spread and his image disappeared. He gathered reeds from the shore and chewed on them. Woodbine and cattails decorated the shore, reminding him of something or someone. The lake cleared and again he peered into the polished surface. Another face behind him peered back.

Who are you? Where do you come from? He pivoted on the balls of his huge feet. He stared at the golden Bigfoot female who hesitated at the edge of the woods. She was beautiful, more lovely than Lally or Torannee. More lovely than he had ever seen. He saw the beauty who had thrown the log at the wild animal which pinned him to the ground. Maybe she was brave and kind. A girl like Mam and Pa had taught him to appreciate.

She bared her teeth and sat down.

"Are there more of you?" His voice sounded like a growl.

It was his own language, but she didn't appear to understand. Of course not. The girl came from Earth. The young female stared at him and played with a handful of grey-green moss. She raised it to her lips, nibbled, and then offered the plant to him. He strode to her side and took the gift. They sat quietly in the warm sunlight without moving. Patches of snow melted around them.

Errl basked in the sun by the side of the lake.

Does she live in the forest? She seems to know how to survive. I can learn. I can teach her my ways and she will teach me hers. I am strong and went to MiddleSchool. I have much to offer, too.

The female Bigfoot bared her teeth again and he smiled back. He ducked his head and plucked a cone from the ground, breaking it open with his teeth and offered it to her. She took it and played with it in her broad silky fingers.

"Eat," he said.

The female shifted her weight, putting her arms around her legs and leaned against his back. Deliciously so. He felt the warmth of the sun. He felt the warmth of her fur against him. His head nodded and he dozed a few minutes in the clearing by the sparkling lake. Then a noise far out on the water woke him.

The female lifted her head, too, and sniffed the air. He smelled the tang of fresh cold water, the lushness of cattails and honeysuckle, and a scent he recognized as human.

A small wooden craft floated on the other side of the lake. A figure bent and rowed, trailing a line behind him.

Interesting. What's he doing out here?

Well, he lives here sometimes, in the building made of sticks.

Errl realized they couldn't be far from the cabin. He felt a coolness at his back and turned his head. The golden girl had disappeared into the forest. A wind sprang up, rippling the surface of the lake and sending chills along his spine. His hair stood on end and he melted into the forest behind the girl.

Kind trapper or man who had sent Errl behind bars? He wasn't sure. He wasn't taking any chances and followed the girl deeper into the woods. She darted amongst the fir trees, the wind moaning in the upper branches.

Good berries. He stopped to harvest more food. Sasquatch could run long and hard. The girl was running now. He began to trot, but lost her as she veered from sight over a small rise then hit the ground on the other side running hard. He could hear the thud of her feet against frozen ground here where the sun didn't warm the earth. He felt good. His thick pelt protected him from the wind. The sickness had left his body and left him warm and cozy. He broke into a run, listening to the thud of the girl's feet about two hundred feet in front of him. He crested the rise of the small hill and began to slide down the other side.

Wood splintered and crashed. The girl screamed once and fell through the rotten timbers into a hole.

He saw it all.

What is it? What happened, so fast in the forest, what is that hole in the floor of the forest? It was manmade, he knew, a trap for wild animals. A trap which had captured his true love.

Errl sprinted to the edge of the hole and grasped the broken and twisted timbers with his huge strong hands; tore them away from the opening. He could hear the girl gasp and cry at the bottom of the pit. He put both hairy paws on the sides, which were littered with limp dead leaves, and peered down into the darkness below. His eyes saw dimly for Sasquatch but good enough to make out the golden female below, twisted and crying. There was snow and ice and a bit of water beneath her, as well as splintered logs and branches. She had fallen through the rotten logs that covered the hole and couldn't climb back out. Her face lifted upward to his. Her eyes pleaded for help. She held her twisted leg.

Is it broken? You are hurt. I'll get you out of there, my love.

He stood up, put his chin into one huge hand and scratched it. Then he scratched his head, looking around for a way to get the girl out of the cave-in without hurting her more.

What would Pa do? What would Teach and Berndt say?

The voices of his friends clamored in his mind. He stilled them. He could do this himself. He poked his head over the side of the well again.

"Stay there. I'll be back."

She doesn't understand. But she became calmer. He soothed her with his voice, growling words she could not possibly understand. He bared his teeth and braced himself against a good sized tree that didn't seem rotten. It broke free. He lowered the log to the bottom of the hole, careful not to let it touch the golden female. It made a kind of bridge up the side of the hole to the top. He climbed down carefully as she watched him.

Is it broken? He crawled beside her and cradled her in his arms. She leaned her head against his broad shoulder. He remembered what Teach had taught them about injuries. *What had he said? Don't move the broken limb?* But Sasquatch's bones were strong, much stronger than humans. Teach had taught them how strong, and what to do. Maybe the leg wasn't broken. The female whimpered and touched the thick golden fur, the twisted leg, then carefully straightened her limb. There wasn't a snap. Teach had said that was a good sign. Errl sighed.

Don't have to set the leg with branches like Teach said. Don't have to take her to cabin.

Humans broke their bones so easily, Teach had said, if they corner you with guns, run. If they set dogs on you, throw the dogs against the trees. If all else fails, break a bone.

The girl's leg wasn't broken. She smiled at him, bared her teeth, grunted and thanked him with her flinty brown eyes that were so lovely, like Lally's but more lovely than anything or anyone he had ever seen. He swept her into his arms and carried her up the log bridge, careful not to hurt her or drop her. She threw her long blonde arms around his neck and snuggled against his shoulder.

I don't want this to end, he thought, but they soon reached the top and he placed her on a bed of soft leaves. Remembering the stinging plant, he checked first, but no stinging plant spread its burning surfaces to irritate her lovely skin.

She lay in his arms in the woods and he gazed down at her. He brushed the golden hair from her lovely flint brown eyes.

Thank you.

What had she said?

"Thank you."

It was human talk. She could speak! With difficulty, but English was now their common language.

"What is your name?" he asked.

"You jerk," she cried, scrabbling to her feet. One last look and she was gone.

Chapter Eighteen

Errl thought it must be his fault his golden girl ran away. *I must have been clumsy or rude.* She would have stayed if he'd been stronger, kinder, more like the Bigfoot she knew.

His sense of direction was poor, but he knew the trapper's cabin was close. He was tired and hungry again. The trapper would have food and a cot in his cabin. If he waited, he was sure the Bigfoot girl would come back.

She's too good for me, anyway.

He sniffed the air. Was that peppermint and fruit he smelled, and something sweet? He followed his nose to the clearing he knew well. Joe Locke and his son weren't there, but they were his friends, weren't they? They would say, *Errl, help yourself to our food and blankets. Help yourself to the water.*

Errl pushed open the plank door.

Mmmm big green fruit with seeds inside, good and like water running down Errl's chin. Cold and yummy. They must be coming back soon. Fruit don't last long. Won't last long with Errl around. He made a noise like hammers on steel, laughed, and found a bag of the sweet things. F-U-D-G-E C-O-O-K-I-E-S, he spelled from the bag like Teach had taught them. *Mmmm good. Cookies.*

A kettle of water, still hot, was on the stove. He knew how to make tea. He sniffed the tins of peppermint and chamomile, then chose peppermint, poured the hot water into a pot with a handful of leaves and drank. *Mmmmmm*

Something sweet. He peered at the jar. H-O-N-E-Y. He poured the golden liquid into a dish and dipped his hand in it, smeared it into his mouth and on his face. *Mmmmmm* Then he fell asleep on a pile of blankets on the floor. He wasn't hungry anymore and there was plenty for later. What a good day.

He awoke with a start. The sun was pouring through the small dirty window over the sink and something was tickling his face. He heard *skitch skratch skootch* and saw a very small animal with whiskers, nose bobbling up and down, smelling his beard.

Food, the creature thought.

What's that? You very small thing, you can think?

Creatures think. Mmmm, food on face. Like bees make in jar.

Bees?

Man comes back soon. skitch skratch skootch and the creature scurried to a hole in the wall.

Come back.

Silence. Then a small grey pointed nose from the hole. *I'm scared.*

Of Errl?

You big man. Scared of man, too. Skitch skratch skootch and the nose disappeared back into the hole.

He thought for a moment. *Are you hungry?*

Man call me mouse.

Come back. Bigfoot boy was lonely. He wanted to play with the mouse.

How come you're here if you're scared?

Food and my children. Here.

Errl thought some more. *I have Pa and Mam.*

Skitch skratch skootch The mouse scampered close to his blankets. *Food.*

"I have food for you." He tried Bigfoot talk. He sounded like a dozen drums falling off a cliff. The mouse ran back to the hole.

Come back.

He got up and shoved his big hand into the bag of F-U-D-G-E C-O-O-K-I-E-S. He broke one, put half into his mouth and sprinkled the bits that were left in front of the hole.

Thank you. The mouse and another grey creature just like it dragged the pieces back to their home. Only crumbs were left on the floor. The mouse came back and inhaled the crumbs, sweeping the floor clean.

My castle is your castle, he thought in his own language, meaning, of course, something much different. He heard noises outside in the forest, noises which he would not have heard if someone or something hadn't meant him to hear. He smiled, baring his huge yellow teeth. He smelled woodbine and crushed cattails. She was watching him.

Let her be alone outside if that's what she wants.

There was a rustle in the forest then silence. Then footsteps.

The door opened. "Hello, Errl," the trapper said. "We've been worried about you."

"Hello, Joe."

He was so disappointed, he wanted it to be the girl.

Meanwhile, his Mam and Pa were on the big spaceship circling Jupiter, plotting ways to get Errl back.

"How can you have let him out of your sight, Dr. Teach?" His Mam peered over Teach's shoulder. "Are you sure he'll meet us?"

"These are the graphs," Teach said. "He has his chronometer."

"Does he have his tech compass? I bet not," Pa growled. "I know the boy. Not a brain in his head."

"Errl will meet us, I just know it," Berndt said. "I can tell you which way he went when I saw him last."

"He'll be lonely, cold and alone. Pa says we'll bring him back to the city and enroll him in army cadets. Our son doesn't belong in MiddleSchool." Teach hung his massive head. Mam massaged Pa's back.

"Have a sweet gummy cud, Missus? We'll find the young sir if he's anywhere close." Teach forgot Errl's name and called him young sir. Berndt rolled his eyes.

"Errl is my best friend. What time did you tell him we'd be there?"

Teach scratched his huge head. He adjusted the vision aids which perched on his small ears. "I can't remember."

"Torannee?" Berndt appealed to Errl's sister.

She groomed the bright blue hair on her belly. "I remember Teach said ten days, six chronos."

Mam sighed. "Good girl, Torannee. We're proud of you." She darted an accusing look at Teach.

"Because of our schedule it can't be less than ten days. It's going to be a scramble to get there on time from other side of moon. Would overshoot Earth if we used star hyperdrive. Must plan for six chronos to meet Errl. There are two Terra days left. We still have solar system to drive through, with no star hyperdrive. We'll get to the moon in a solar day, but have to wait there to beam up wrecking crew."

Will we make it? Berndt rolled his eyes again and looked at Teach. Mam and Pa huddled with Torannee and Lally.

"We must call the Captain and get the airpod ready for two loops of the moon around the earth, at six chronos. The big ship will wait on the dark side of the moon doing experiments, 253,000 miles out in space. Screens have to be up and cloaked."

"Uhhh...problem with small airpod, tractor beam doesn't work right."

The beam that would bring Errl up to the airpod from Earth.

"The hypertechs are working on it, Missus most Revered," Berndt said. "They don't quite know what's wrong. But we've got two Solar days to get it working."

"The thing never did work right," Pa said. "How do we know it's going to beam our son up properly?"

One of the hypertechs spun around in his chair at the control console. "We need better numbers than our computers can give us," he said. "We're working against time."

"Can't something be done?"

"We're needed somewhere else," said the hypertech. "We've spent enough time on it."

"What about our son?"

"He is one Bigfoot amongst billions."

"Sacrifice the one for the many? No, not our Errl. We trusted you, Dr. Teach. We trusted the MiddleSchool Captain to get him to Earth and back safely."

"Doesn't always happen," the tech said. "Sorry, we can't do any more."

Teach pulled the long hairs on both sides of his face, brows wrinkling. He sat in front of the teaching machines and bowed his head.

Then his hands flew over the controls.

Neon bright symbols flashed across the screen. Teach stopped once to drink a Vskian energy juice, banged the container down on the control desk and his webbed fingers flew. He grunted once, not satisfied.

"What's wrong?" Mam held her breath. It all depended on Teach and his higher education.

"Nothing. Glitch going too fast, nobody's done this before," Teach muttered. Symbols flashed. The room grew dark, then a blueprint of the airpod appeared on the screen, tracking numbers assigned to each portion, perfectly aligned.

"I'll be tied in Zorster's toenails, Teach got it working right." Lally laughed with a sound like dishes breaking in a *Vskia Vestapixital* restaurant.

Joe Locke slopped the bucket of fish into the sink. He covered Errl with a blanket as the Bigfoot slept on the floor.

"Sleep, big fella," he said. "You deserve it."

Errl bared his teeth and huddled on top of the pile of blankets. He smiled in his sleep. The smell of woodbine and crushed cattails was stronger in his nostrils than the smell of fish.

She's waiting for me out there, in the woods.

He woke up once and could hardly wait till morning. He checked his chronometer. Teach wouldn't lie. Day seven, coming up eight. Right. Countdown started now.

I'm free. It won't be long before I see my own ship. Nobody will find me here. This is a safe place.

The cabin was not a safe place, of course. Joe knew that. He worried about his son and about Errl. He knew the hunters would not give up. The RCMP always got their man. The town of Parsnip Creek hated strangers and feared aliens. The Cub leader, Peter Puffin, had seen Errl's airship go down. Reporters would come from all over the world. Doctors would poke and probe the Bigfoot boy.

I'm free, Errl thought, but Joe knew better.

Chapter Nineteen

"Yeah, we saw him, officer." The young teen grinned. They were standing at the counter in the police station in Cranbrook.

"We followed him," another teen said. "He went into the bush near Parsnip Creek. There's a trapper's cabin up there, isn't there?"

"Sure is. It's a place of interest to us," the female officer said. "What do you boys know about the Bigfoot?"

"Only that he escaped."

"Only that he's wanted."

"Only that there oughta be a reward for his capture, ma'am."

"Is that so?" The officer swung around to her computer screen. "It says here no reward, boys."

"What?"

"Why did we bother following the dude, then?"

"What's your name, boys?" Then the teens thought better of their plan. "Hmmm. Never mind, ma'am."

Her forehead wrinkled. "There was a situation out at the Miette highway near Kamloops reported to us this morning. A vanload of teens assaulted an officer's horse and got away."

"A horse? Assaulted a horse?" The teens snorted behind their hands. "Kind of a farfetched story, isn't it, officer?"

"No, not really. Our boys were pulling three fine horses in a trailer behind a police van that broke down. Story is four teens…" She stopped, aware she was giving out classified information.

"Story, yeah." The boys shifted their weight. One hitched up his jeans. "Well, we'll be going now."

"Just a minute."

"Who's that? Young Puffin?" A male Mountie entered the room with a sheaf of papers in his hand. He flicked through them. "Isn't your dad looking for you, young Puffin? He's mighty strict, I think. Wouldn't want to see his son and three hoods messing up his new van, either, would he now?"

"Uh, no, sir." The teen spat in an ashtray. "We were just going."

"I'm not young Puffin," the other said. "You must have me mixed up with somebody else."

"Wait."

"You can't hold us. We know our rights."

"Yeah, we come in to do a good thing. Report the Bigfoot."

"The Bigfoot your dad is hunting?"

"We'll go now."

The policeman stepped in front of them. The female officer made a phone call.

"Pete? Come down here and get your son. Isn't far from Parsnip Creek, shouldn't take you long."

"Judge will set bail in the morning," the male officer said. He took young Puffin's arm and herded the others into the back.

The teens laughed.

"We'll get released as soon as my dad gets here," Taylor Puffin said. "He's a big fish in a small pond."

His dad came twenty minutes later. They were released.

"Bigfoot never hurt anybody," the female officer said, after Peter Puffin had left with the boys in his custody.

"Yeah, I feel real bad about the whole thing," replied the other Mountie. "Our boys are on their way back from Miette with the three horses and no prisoner. They're gonna be ticked we let the teens get away, too."

"That Herman is a thing of beauty and a boy forever."

"Would you like a coffee, Jean?"

"Don't mind. It's gonna be a long night."

"Yeah, a long night for Bigfoot, too, if he's out in the woods. He must know enough not to go near that trapper's cabin. But we'll send somebody up there in the morning just in case."

"It's a big lot of bush to hide in. If we were serious we'd put out an all points bulletin. But we just got that crazy story of Pete's and the reporters bugging us. We should let the poor guy go."

"Yeah, or at least wait until he's done something really wrong."

"Yes." She frowned and pinched her lower lip. "That's the trouble. He might do something really wrong."

"I think that's the problem all right."

"Okay, let's send the sheriff in Parsnip Creek up there with his deputy tomorrow. They can question the trapper, too."

"Joe Locke?"

"He seems like a nice enough guy."

"Soft for the Bigfoot, and soft for his young boy. Boy's having trouble at school, I hear."

"That's just gossip from Parsnip Creek, comes from Pete and his good ol' boys. I think they'd take the law in their hands if they had half a chance."

"Already have."

"There's an election coming up. Have to remember that, Jean."

"Shouldn't have anything to do with us."

"No. Shouldn't."

The two officers locked the doors and went in the back to share sandwiches and coffee.

Errl didn't know his new teen friends had tried to betray him.

It was the end of the seventh day.

Chapter Twenty

You are great. You are so great. You're better than Zombie candy. You're better than Zorster brains.

She peeked out from the forest in the morning. Errl couldn't believe his senses. The smell of heady woodbines. The reek of crushed cattails. The soft plush golden fur of a *zammot* kitten, the siren wail of a mountain girl not yet tamed, eyes brown and flinty, ears close to the head like velvet gloves, soft broad webbed hands which fluttered like flags in salute, and she was smaller than Torannee and Lally, smaller than his Mam, more importantly, much smaller than him.

His soul-mate, though the girl didn't know it yet. His own true love.

He was smitten.

Staring at this vision, he stood by the trapper's cabin. She began to run. He followed.

With great loping steps he overtook her.

"Stop. I want to talk to you."

She growled and wailed, music of the forest. She continued to run, looking over her gorgeous golden shoulders as she ran. He followed, oh, he followed, the pads on his feet blistered and sore, his hair matted again from sleeping on the floor, his eyes bright and his mouth laughing foolishly as he followed her.

You won't get away.

She stopped finally, panting, turned and faced him.

He leaned against a tree, peeled the bark from a root with his toes, grinned and reached out to stroke her smooth back.

She flew into him, both fists flailing, mouth wide with a scream that could be heard all the way into town. The men with the guns paid attention, then readied their hounds.

"Stop." He rolled on the ground, she on top of him, striking his head over and over with her great soft fists. She growled again and tore chunks of fur from his belly. They rolled through the litter of dead leaves on the forest floor. They rolled over through frozen mud and chunks of winter grey ice. He protected his eyes with his arms and pummeled her chest. She screamed and bit him.

"Stop."

I don't know your name. I just want to know you. Why are you doing this? You are my own true love. Haven't you figured that out? Can't you see it when you look at me?

She began to tickle him. Surprised, he laughed and pulled her hands away. She brought her great gentle lips to his face and kissed him, laughing, then pulled away again and they rolled in one another's embrace to the bottom of the hill, to the plank door of the trapper's cabin, and there they lay panting while Joe Locke gazed at them in astonishment from inside his door.

"Oh, so you've come back," was all the trapper could say.

"He's brought a friend!" Joey laughed and poked Errl. "You must be hungry after that adventure."

Errl and the female shook the dead leaves from their fur and stood up. She glanced sideways at him and showed her teeth.

"Me, too," he said to her. "I liked it, too."

Joe Locke and Joey were grinning.

"We brought medical supplies," Joey said. "And fruit and cupcakes and pizza. We can bake the pizza in our camp stove here."

Joe looked at Errl's sore feet. "These need tending to," he said. "Right away. Your feet are bruised and bleeding, Errl, and you've lost some weight. Actually, you look pretty fit compared to the big soft teddy bear I met a few days ago. How did you get away, pal? Last we saw of you, you were in an armored truck heading for the coast hundreds of miles away. You are one amazing humongous bunny."

"I go home," Errl said.

"You came home? That's great." Joey slapped him on the back, then stopped. "Wait a minute. You don't mean us, do you? You want to go back to your friends on the space ship. Of course you do. Poor fellow, you're lonely."

He put his arm around the female's shoulders. "Not lonely no more," he said.

She hit him hard on the chest. He laughed and fell over. She ran back into the forest.

"She'll be back," the trapper said. He beckoned Errl inside and began to wash his sore muddy feet. Joey gave him a comb and a mirror.

"Need cloth to wash my face," Errl said.

"Oh, really? Suddenly vain, are we?" Joe Locke grinned and provided the moist warm cloth and a hot towel warmed over the camp stove.

Errl growled and showed his teeth.

"Oh, we are pleased with ourselves, aren't we?"

"Dad." Joey stopped slicing fruit. "I hear the dogs and the sounds of the ATVs. They're coming this way."

"They must have heard the ruckus."

"Quick, Errl, into this closet. It's a tight fit but there's air and it's warm and dry. Just until they leave. Please?"

Joe swept the footsteps from the front of the cabin with a long handled broom and a shovel. Joey cleaned the mud and blood from the basin of water and rinsed out the cloth and towels. They began to whistle. They were enjoying pizza and fruit when Peter Puffin and his friends pulled up outside the door in their All Terrain Vehicles.

"All right, Joe." The sheriff got out of his truck and hitched up his pants. He peered into the cabin. "Where is he?"

"Who?"

"Don't play dumb with us, Locke. We know he's here."

"Don't know what you're talking about, Pete. Jeff."

The men circled the cabin. Puffin sniffed the air.

"I can smell him."

"My boy and I came up for the day to check the trap lines. Maybe what you're smelling is good old muskrat."

"Or Bigfoot." They circled the cabin again.

There was a grunt from the closet.

"What's that?"

"What?"

"I heard something. My dog here smells something, too. Look at him. You got him in the closet, Locke." Puffin cocked his rifle.

My one true love.

From the forest erupted a ball of golden fur, wild in nature, she screamed and crashed through the trees in front of the men. They grabbed their guns and gave chase. The hounds followed.

"There he is! The Bigfoot. He looks different now that he's had a chance to groom himself." The female looked behind and slowed her pace. She zigzagged through the forest, farther and farther away. The ATVs roared to action, soon outdistancing the hounds.

No.

"No, Errl. Don't follow her. She'll get away when they realize they've got the wrong Bigfoot. Let her be brave for you, buddy. She's saving your life. It's you they want, not her. They'll find out soon enough she's no alien and they'll let her go back to the forest where they know she belongs. She's a treasure, but not to Peter Puffin. They're all after you, the big sky Bigfoot. You're the one they'll analyze and put away for good. It's not her they want, I promise you, Errl. Don't worry, she'll get away. They won't guard her closely. She's a smart bunny and the sheriff is on our side."

No. My true love.

But the men had caught her. She looked back once before getting in the back of the truck, dogs nipping at her heels. Then she was gone.

Chapter Twenty-One

"Boy, they're stupid. She doesn't look anything like you, Errl."

"I want a gummy wad."

"Errl, we've been through this before. We don't have any gummy wads. We don't even have any gum."

"Yes, you do. Friend boys gave me gummy wad yesterday."

"What friend boys? That doesn't sound good. You must be dreaming."

"She won't come back."

"Sure, pal, she'll come back. The sheriff isn't that much of a dweeb. He knew it wasn't you. The others will realize it soon enough. They'll hold her for awhile then let her go back into the wilds where she belongs."

"I want to go home."

"You can go home, buddy. We know how to get you home. The Cub leader told us where they saw the airship go down. It's just over there, not more than a couple or three hours walk through dense bush. First Nations people told us about strange happenings there by the river, a big circle where a fire ship took off, something dark around the moon coming this way. It's not long now. Ten loops around the earth, you say? That would be just a couple days from now, if I'm not mistaken."

"Want to go home."

"Here. Look at this, pal." Joey bent and made marks in the frozen earth with a pointed stick. "Here, this is us, okay? And this is the river. This is the edge of the forest. This is where your ship went down."

"Really?" He checked his chronometer. "Ship will come back at six chronos tomorrow."

"If I'm right, that's about four o'clock our time. If we leave at noon we'll get there in lots of time."

"Don't want to leave without pretty golden girl."

"We'll have to think on that. Might not be easy to spring her now that you've gotten away from them. Twice bitten twice shy, you know."

"They know she's not me?"

"They must. You don't look alike."

"All Bigfoot look alike to stupid men."

"True."

"Hairy and big." He hung his head. "But she's a beautiful Bigfoot. I am ugly. What does she see in me?"

"You're quite the catch, I would think," Joe Locke said. "Boy Bigfoot from the stars, bright, educated, handsome in a rugged way. When your wounds heal." He smiled.

The picture the human drew in the mud is right. I remember the river, the forest, the clearing in the forest, the stars and the moon the way they were that night when I ran away from the Cub leader.

"I can go home."

"Yes."

"I will stay here."

"What?"

"I won't leave the golden girl."

"She'll be all right. I promise you."

"She will come with me or I will stay here. They won't let her go in time for the walk back to my ship. I won't leave without her."

"Be reasonable, Errl." Joe wiped his face with a bandanna he wore around his neck. "All this for nothing?"

"They will punish her."

"They won't. I promise. The sheriff is a good man. He'll let her go. They know she's no alien. She belongs here, in the woods."

"With me."

"You belong in the stars," Joe said.

"I will take her with me or I will stay here."

"You are one stubborn Bigfoot."

"Yes. I am stubborn."

"What if she doesn't want to go with you?"

"Then I wait for her to tell me that."

"She can't even speak your language. You can't speak hers. How do you expect to talk to each other?"

"We talk the language of love."

"You're impossible."

"Yes. I'm impossible."

It was the eighth day, and as the white moon rose over the little cabin in the woods, Errl heard a sound that was like his very favorite music rise up from the forest below.

The female Bigfoot was wailing, on her way on the trail to the cabin, and wafted before her was the odor of woodbine and crushed cattails.

"She came back."

"The sheriff must have let her go."

"I will call her Hunny Bear," Errl said and smiled.

"That sounds like an Earth name," Joey said.

"Yes. I know. She will like it."

"I like the sheriff," Joey said.

"You can't trust him, son." The trapper drummed his fingers on the table and watched Errl and Hunny in the forest holding hands. "Come in," he called. "They'll be after you in the morning."

Chapter Twenty-Two

Before the sun rose the next morning Errl and Hunny had left the cabin. They wandered through the forest to a broad highway and crossed it. Green Lake was on one side, the mountain on the other. He helped her climb the side of the mountain and from there it was an easy jog to Crowfoot, which she knew.

"Sasquatch won't go into town," she warned. He looked around. They crouched in Schneider's Campground on the outskirts of Crowfoot. Campers stirred the embers of fires from the morning, others packed up to leave. Mr. Schneider sat in his office and read the morning papers from Calgary and Vancouver.

All was quiet.

Errl peered from a small patch of woods in the campground. "Wow! Hunny Bear, look at this."

"Not Hunny Bear."

"Hunny girl. My golden girl. Look at this. Big hairy Bigfoot in yard across road."

"Yes, I know." They grunted together, sounding like gravel crunching beneath the tires of the brewery trucks opposite the campground.

"Wow, box in his hand, stands twelve, fourteen feet tall, humans would say."

"Sasquatch make beer for Kranberg brewery."

"How you know this, Hunnybunch?"

"Hunny been here before many times. Like Sasquatch statue."

"That's a statue?"

"Sure, silly Errl. Made out of stone."

"Holy Zorster's webbed feet."

"Yes, let's go see up close."

"Wow, that one's big!"

"Hunny maybe stay here. Bad luck to be seen."

"Oh, I'm not shy," he said. He put a big foot out in the morning sun, away from the shelter of trees.

"Go across road." She bared her teeth and pushed him.

"You sure?"

"Hunny sure."

Errl crossed the road.

He stood at the foot of the Sasquatch mascot. It carried a box of Kranberg beer in its huge hand. That's big! he thought. I not a small human. But why they worship Sasquatch here? He scratched his head. A short distance away there was a wooden cut-out of a Sasquatch with a hole where its face should be. What could that be used for by these very strange humans? He stood still. The morning broke apart for him when a couple dressed in very bright floral shirts with cameras around their necks—spoke to him from not far away!

"Look, George, isn't that cute? A guy dressed up like a Sasquatch. What will they think of next?"

"Hey, fella, can y'all come over here and stand still fer a picture? We got nothing like this in Phoenix, Arizona. Wait'll Mildred and Fred see these pictures. I'll give you an American twenty dollar bill if y'all will let us take yer picture."

Errl made a noise like bricks falling from a height and bared his teeth.

Mam won't believe this.

He stood by the Sasquatch statue for a picture and accepted the twenty dollar bill. He waved both arms while the woman stuck her head through the wooden cut-out in front of the brewery.

"George, now it's yer turn."

A man ran out of the building next to the cut-out and yelled. His eyes were wide. Errl bolted for the road and hid again in Schneider's Campground. Hunny hugged him. Two sets of eyes were wide and watched the couple from Arizona struggle with the man from the brewery.

"Isn't he one of yours?" The woman put her hand to her mouth.

"No, never saw the creature before in my life."

"Where'd he get that costume?" George snapped a picture of his wife with the employee in front of the cut-out. Errl heard an engine start up near the brewery. He and Hunny disappeared farther into the bushes in Schneider's Campground.

"Lady, that's not a costume. We ain't got no costume like that and nobody here's seven feet tall. That there is a *real* Bigfoot. Wait'll I tell the boss."

George dropped his cigar. "Now, George, we got it all on film. Just you wait till I tell Mildred about this." The man cleared his throat.

"Just got something caught in my throat, Helen."

"Don't be embarrassed, George. That critter's big enough to scare the boots off anybody." She patted George's arm.

"You really made our day, sweetums," she called out to Errl as he melted into the woods.

"Hunny go home," his girl said, ever the fickle partner.

"No, don't leave Errl. Errl lonely."

"This not Hunny's home," she said. "You all right now, Bigfoot Boy. I leave you now. You come back to cabin in one day, we go to river together. We find airship. Right? You must hide now. They search for you. Hunny not safe with Errl."

He went on alone, into the backwoods near the temples of the religious fathers that dotted the area, farther into the countryside around Crowfoot.

Chapter Twenty-Three

"Look, Jessie, it's a Magnolia Warbler," the birder whispered. "I see it through the trees."

"Rare in these parts this time of year," his companion hissed. "Blackish above with white eyebrow, yellow rump, white tail patches, yellow underneath. Yes, you're right, Bert. What a find!" She adjusted her binoculars. "What's that he's perched on? A hairy tree?"

"My gosh, Jessie, it's a hairy beast!"

"Should we take a picture of the beast or the bird, Bert?" His companion fumbled with her notepad and camera.

"I don't know. This is very unusual."

Errl stood very still. The bird wobbled on his shoulder.

weety-weety-weeteo

What's that you say, little feathered creature?

Moist coniferous forest. Ideal for me.

What are you?

I fly.

Like airpod?

weety-weety-weeteo. Humans expect no less.

There are humans here?

Look ahead.

Oh, no. He wondered if he should run or approach the humans.

"Jessie, can you locate it in"Field Guide to Birds of America?"

"Yes, of course. It's right here. This is the Magnolia Warbler, winters in Mexico or Florida, West Indies, we're so lucky to find it here. What a wonderful morning!"

"There's something else there."

"Well, yes. The Bigfoot."

"That isn't a small thing."

"No, well, you're the reporter, Bert. Why don't you take a picture for your paper?"

"I'll do better than that. Do we have enough pictures of the Warbler?"

"I think so. Here, let me jot this all down, date, time, location, weather, appearance."

"Yes, yes. I have it here on my Sony Notepad, too. I'll just text the cops in Parsnip Creek with our location."

"Why?"

"This Bigfoot is wanted. He's a fugitive from the law."

"What did he do?"

"Well, nothing, I guess. He's just…unusual."

"That doesn't seem like reason to snitch on him. He looks kind of cute. The Warbler likes him and trusts him."

"Yes…" Bert was uneasy. "Well, maybe I'll let him go. Poor thing."

Errl stood still with the bird on his arm. Then he realized the danger he was in from the humans, the possibility of humans hunting him…and Hunny…he jerked around and the bird flew away. Bert and Jessie moved closer, pinpointing their location with the GPS on Bert's Notepad. Jessie snapped more pictures. Errl gave them the American twenty dollar bill.

"Oh, that's kind of nice. Look what he gave me. We're not afraid, are we, Bert?" she asked.

"Nope."

He knew the camera and Notepad could signal the hunters to pick him up, put him back in jail, maybe even take him on the road again. He lunged closer to the humans. He grabbed the camera from Jessie and pulled on the Notepad. Bert held on tight and swore.

"Brown sugar, the creature is savage."

"Bert, I'm scared."

"Run, Jess!" Bert pulled and the Notepad came away in his hand. Errl held the bright cover. Bert ran with his companion through the trees. The twenty dollar bill fluttered down and was ground into the frozen leaves.

"My camera, Bert."

"I still have mine. The creature might be after us. Faster! I have my Notepad."

"Call for help."

"I can't call for help and run at the same time, woman."

They looked behind. The creature was gone. They could hear his footsteps crashing through the forest and then silence.

"He finally did it. He committed his first crime. We have it all on camera."

"Bert, I'm real scared."

"That's all right. The RCMP just answered me. They're sending out a posse to this area right now. They're sure to take him in if he doesn't get out of the area. He roughed us up a bit, didn't he?"

"Well, yeah, I guess so."

"He broke your camera. That expensive piece of equipment."

"Yeah, he did."

"He's a bad creature, Jess."

"Yeah, I guess he is."

Now Errl was truly a fugitive. He continued to run, hoping to outrun his tormentors. Hoping to get home. This was the middle of the eighth day. He must get back to the river. He must rejoin Hunny at the cabin.

Chapter Twenty-Four

Errl was hungry and tired. He ran through the forest away from the village of Crowfoot. He ate twigs, berries and moss, drank water from the many streams and a small lake. His feet hurt. The Bigfoot finally stumbled into a farmyard.

I won't hurt you.

The cows, seeing the large furry creature, bolted with tails high toward the other end of the hayfield. Some crashed through a barbed wire fence and ran into the forest, bleeding from cuts. The horses whinnied and reared. The chickens and turkeys squawked and fluttered. A pen of pigs grunted and stared.

"You stay right there, boy. I seen you on TV."

The farmer recognized Errl as a wanted fugitive. He stopped with a pail of mash in his hand and a pitchfork in the other. The farmer meant to feed his pigs and horses. A bucket of grain sat on the ground near the wooden slats of a fence.

"You scared all my animals away, you furry critter. I don't believe you meant to. You look a right sorry sight."

Errl kept his eyes on the farmer and scooped some grain from the bucket. He gulped it down, hardly stopping to chew. The farmer approached the Bigfoot with his bucket of mash and some corn, meant for the pigs.

"Here, pal. Have some of this."

A kind human but the last humans seemed kind. They chased me and said bad things.

Errl came closer and grabbed the pail, taking it to a corner of the yard and gorged himself. The farmer watched.

"You want a warm place to stay tonight? Feels like snow."

A cold wind blew from the north. Clouds scudded across the scarlet sun.

"You can stay in my barn. My Pa won't be home till morning. We won't hurt you."

"Barn?" The farmer could hear only grunts and sighs. Errl climbed up the loft and covered himself with hay. Frost rimmed the edge of the hay pile. The farmer went back to his house. Errl saw a light come on and a single figure sat at a table. He grunted.

Wait till Pa comes home. Man has Pa? Like Errl.

He slept.

Errl woke to hear heavy footsteps in the barn below. He peeked through a hole in the hayloft. An older human hooked up machines to the cows, which were snorting and pawing. They could smell Errl.

"What's the matter with you all?" The human looked around. "Is something spooking you, Bessie?"

Oooooom.

I won't hurt you, Bessie.

Oooooom.

"Time to check the pigeons in the loft." He could hear someone climbing a ladder to the hole. He covered himself again with hay. The footsteps continued to the back of the loft. Birds cooed.

Tweeeeet tweeeet cooo cooo

I won't hurt you.

Human very good.

"My pigeons look okay. Nothing up here to be scared of, Bess." The man's footsteps echoed on the plank floor. Errl heard sounds of some- one climbing down the ladder. The cows lowed.

Then all was quiet.

Errl waited.

Is it safe to leave?

Ooooooom.

I won't hurt you.

He threw the straw off his hairy body and lumbered toward the ladder. When he stood on the floor of the barn the animals all spooked. The horses lunged against their stables and the cows snorted and bellowed. He could hear the pigs squeal outside in their pen. He scooped up a handful of mash and corn then ran out the back. He could hear the farmer's Pa yelling and running toward the barn. He could hear the farmer trying to calm his animals.

"That's all right, Blue, Bessie, Joybelle. That's all right. Whoa now, Blackie. Good boy."

I'm scared. This is a strange new world all right. Humans are very strange. Some are friendly. Some scream and run. Strange new world.

Errl scratched his head and melted into the forest.

I'm used to running in the woods now. The pads on my feet are tougher and thicker.

Behind him, the sounds of the barnyard grew faint. The farmer had been kind. He hadn't given the farmer's Pa a chance to be kind. Maybe the man didn't mean to hurt Errl? But Errl couldn't be sure. He ran and ran.

Thumpa Thumpa

He was beginning to enjoy himself. He hummed as he ran through the forest back to Hunny and Trapper Joe, on the eighth day. He sounded like a buzz saw cutting through timber.

A posse was after him. *Thumpa Thumpa* At nightfall he reached the road near Goose Lake and then, the cabin.

Chapter Twenty-Five

He stumbled onto the road and there was the van with the teens. They stopped to pick him up. Errl had friends.

How'd you know I was here?

They didn't know, he thought. Zorster was on his side with his demons and angels and the great god looking after Pa's son.

"Yee haw." Puffin's son clapped him on the back. "Hello, pal."

"Yes."

"You want to go to a party, chum?"

"Yes." He settled into the back of the van. One of the teens opened a window. He took a deep breath of the cool air that rushed through. One of the teens gagged.

"Eeyah."

"We're on our way to Goose Lake. Sun's going down. Perfect night for a fire and a party. Cola drink, Bigfoot?"

"Thank you." He accepted the can of soda pop. He drank it and burped. Good. Almost as good as the cola Joey had shared with him days ago. The van careened down the highway, swerving to avoid cars that shot by every now and then. They turned off onto a logging road, then continued near Goose Lake. Puffin's son stopped the van at a clearing in the firs.

"We're here."

"Where?" He didn't understand. The woods were dark. The lake shone silver under a full moon. He looked up. Was the airship on its way to him? One of the teens gave him a can of *Wacked Bison Sports Drink*. He gulped it, thinking it was soda pop. He began to feel dizzy.

"Big party," said one of the girls crammed in the van. They piled out into the clearing and lit a fire.

"Hotdogs, marshmallows, S'mores," the girls said. "Here, Jamie, I've brought my guitar. Susan's brought her harmonica."

"Good, we can have a sing-a-long." The boys paired up with the girls. Errl watched.

Wish Hunny was here. I would put my arm around her, too.

The night grew late.

"Guess our parents will miss us?"

"Dad will be mad."

There was laughter, drinking, messy mustard and marshmallows and cookies on their faces, Errl smeared S'mores on his hairy face and bared his teeth. Two of the sisters began to sing "Fire Burning" by Sean Kingston. The boys joined in. Errl swayed, grunted, and sang like a bag of crushed car parts crashing together.

The teens laughed. "Posse after you, big fella?"

"Yes." He grunted and bared his teeth again.

"I like the way you laugh," one of the sisters crooned. She reached over and pulled the hair on the side of his face. "You're kind of cute."

"Cut that out, Marty." A boy reached over and added a log to the fire. Flames crackled and jumped in the darkness. Sparks flew. The girls began to sing "Seasons in the Sun."

"My mom says she sang that song when she was a kid."

"No way."

"Yeah, she knows the words and everything."

"No way, it's a different song."

"Probably."

The campfire was only coals. An owl hooted in the woods nearby. Errl shivered. The wind off the lake was cold. Clouds scudded over the moon.

"Looks like maybe snow tomorrow," one of the boys remarked.

"Yeah, it's getting cold. Let's go."

They let him out on the highway into Parsnip Creek. He stumbled a bit in the dark but his eyes, though not sharp, could make out objects in the night better than humans. He saw the sign, "Parsnip Creek" and followed along the side of the road into town. He sat and stared at the lights of town.

This is home.

From far away, an ATV belched thunder.

Maybe not home. It's the sheriff and his humans. He bared his teeth and wandered back to the trapper's cabin where he seemed to be safe.

They never find me there.

He met a cop at the door.

Chapter Twenty-Six

The sergeant was kind. "That's it, Bigfoot boy. Don't you have enough sense to go back to where you came from? We've staked this place out. Shoulda done it sooner but wanted to give you a chance, with ol' Pete after you and his boys and all. Seemed only fair to give you a chance. You didn't do anything wrong until day before yesterday."

Wrong? Oh, yes. Camera guy and rare bird.

"You'll have to come with me, then," the sergeant said. He held a huge tranquilizer gun. A helicopter hovered above. The cabin stood between Errl and his friends Joe Locke and Joey. His friends peered out from the little room with the cot and stove.

Don't be scared for me. I'm not a bad Bigfoot alien guy.

Joey dropped a pan in the kitchen, shattering the silence. The sergeant turned around and Errl moved fast, so fast that the cop didn't have a chance. He ran for the cover of the forest, dodging back and forth as the helicopter pilot took his place and dropped smoke bombs from the sky.

Errl dived into the woods. Where was Hunny?

Hunny stay away. Danger here.

He ran flat out and sure footed, as all Bigfoot could do, dodging trank bullets as he ran. He ran into a place that looked familiar. A place in the woods he and Hunny had met, he was sure. Then... he fell into the pit.

The same pit that Hunny had fallen into, seemingly a year ago. The log was weak. It crushed under his weight and crumbled. He fell; the log striking his head. The last he heard was the helicopter whirling overhead.

Did they see me?

Then blackness.

He came to in the bottom of the pit, sitting in a pool of black water, spiders and rotten branches. Ducked as he heard the 'copter turn around again, but the sound grew fainter, searching another part of the forest.

They didn't see me fall into the hole. But how do I get out? Maybe I'm safer in here for now. They won't find me here. I will wait before I call to Joe Locke for help.

The sun swung overhead and left him in deep shadow in the bottom of the hole. He scratched his head. Good thing there was no snow. Ice crystals formed in the black water he sat in. He shivered, listening to the silence. He could hear Joe and his son calling for him. He tried to call out but no sound came. His head hurt. He was sure he would die in the bottom of that black stagnant pit.

Night fell. Joe and Joey had quit calling. They probably thought he had escaped. He knew they would go back to town. He listened at the sound of the helicopter taking a couple of turns, and watched as the searchlight pierced the dark like an arrow, then it, too, went away. He held his head.

Hunny?

Psst, you big lug. It was her. She reached down and gave him her hand. He took it, weak and dizzy from the knock on the head earlier that day. She tried to haul him up but he was too heavy.

Stand on log.

Errl obeyed. He stood on the log and climbed on all fours as far as he could. The hole was very deep. Poor Hunny had fallen into this very hole. How scared she must have been. He could remember…

Pass me a big branch, Hunny.

She hauled him out. He sat muddy and cold on the edge of the hole. She poked him and laughed like static on an old time radio.

Must board up hole so nobody else falls in. They dragged solid fallen logs over the pit until it was covered. They left for a safer place, Hunny leading.

Where we going, Hunny?

Deep in mountains. Very high in mountain where my people are.

Your people? Errl thought you were alone.

No, I like to come down low where it is warmer and more food. My people high in mountain. They do not come this way. Much bad happen to my people at hands of human.

She led him up and up the mountain. Sometimes they heard strange noises but they kept going. Wild animals did not scare them. Most bears were sleeping. Big cats were not as big or strong as they were. A bird hooted and he glanced behind him. They were very high in the forest, which was thinning. Then...

Hunny's Kinfolk. A tribe of Sasquatch, very like him, bigger than Hunny, black and brown in color, children, too. He stared.

How did you get here?

Long ago, Hunny said in their shared speech. *Long ago my Kinfolk came here from far away.*

Far away like me?

Maybe, Errl. Nobody knows. So long ago.

He stared at the children, only four feet tall, and their mothers and fathers, the uncles and one old silverback grandfather, the leader of them all.

They surrounded Hunny and hugged her, chittering in their own speech, patting her, grooming her, standing back and staring at her.

They thought they wouldn't see you again. Errl was surprised how he knew this. By Zorster's kneecaps, there was something they shared that was without words. He was proud. These could be his people, too.

My Kinfolk will groom you and clean you up, Errl. Let them make you whole again. Your head hurts. Let grandfather Silverback give you some of his medicine.

The old Sasquatch eyed Errl. He chose a plant that grew near the mouth of the cave and chewed it, gazing all the time at him. Then he put the chewed plant on Errl's head.

Don't do that, old grandfather. His head felt cold and tingled at the same time. Then he sat down. His head didn't ache anymore! He felt the soggy fur around his forehead. The wound was healing as he sat there.

I'm so grateful. Thank you, grandfather. I nearly died.

You did not nearly die. But you did hurt your head and you couldn't think or walk straight, my son. We will heal you. We will groom you and clean you and then you will go back to your own Kinfolk.

Errl grunted. He put a hand to the top of his head. The chewed plants soothed his headache. They took away the pain. His wound started to feel better, the skin already healing.

Bigfoot too tough to die from little fall. He felt better all of a sudden and stopped feeling sorry for himself. He would join his own Kinfolk, yes, soon he would hike to the spot where he left his airship, Teach and Berndt and his sister and Lally, and he would leave this odd planet with its many surprises. With its many different surprises every day.

He was so tired of Earth.

Hunny?

A big Sasquatch with a black crown of hair and a brown streak of fur down his dark back stood to one side. He sulked as he watched Hunny.

Oh, oh, Errl thought. A rival.

His chronograph hummed. He looked at it. Two more Terra days. Hunny...he strode to her side and took her hand. She gazed back at the big black Sasquatch but followed Errl down the mountain.

There is no moon tonight.

No.

My Kinfolk will come from the far side of the moon.

When?

In two Terra days.

I will be with you.

Come, Hunny. We must get ready.

Something or someone followed them. Whenever Errl looked back, there was no one there.

Chapter Twenty-Seven

"I left map of how to find my ship at the cabin." Errl spoke in English to Hunny, who seemed to understand.

She growled.

"I know. The humans in uniform have found us there. It isn't safe to go back."

But we must.

"Yes. We must go back. My map. Joe Locke and Joey will be there. They'll show us the way to the big river where my airship will meet us. I've forgotten the way, Hunny."

Trust them?

"Yes. We must trust or the enemy will be happy."

We go through back woods and stay off roads.

"That's good, Hunny." He took her hand. The sun was rising. He didn't hear any ATVs or trucks or helicopters. They ducked under the tall branches of the firs and hid. They padded on quiet big feet to the edge of the clearing where the cabin sat under the morning light. It seemed so quiet.

"Joey?"

"Errl?"

"Joey!"

"Errl!" The boy flung himself into Errl's arms. Then he stopped, face red. "Where have you been? We were so worried."

"Hunny and Errl have been up the mountain. Found other Bigfoot."

"No! Can you show me?"

"Can never show humans." Honey stood in front of Errl, arms crossed in front of her chest. "Errl very bad to tell you."

"Sorry." He hung his head.

Joey patted his arm. "That's all right, pal. I understand. If we humans found out where the rest of the Bigfoot live, well, that would be the end of the Bigfoot, wouldn't it?"

"Yes." Hunny snarled and stood tall as she could.

Hunny loves her Kinfolk. Will she love me more? Will she come with me?

The trapper came up behind Joey.

"Well, hello, Errl. I see your friend came back."

"Yeah, what happened to her, anyhow?" Joey led them to a quiet place in the woods, away from the clearing. Errl thought that was a smart thing to do. He was tired and not thinking right. He had to take care of Hunny, too. His head hurt again. He needed more of that chewed plant. Hunny?

No more of medicine. Grandfather Silverback has all the medicine. We would have to stay there, Errl.

"The Mounties didn't find you." Joey puffed out his chest. "I got such a smart Bigfoot friend."

"I fell in hole in ground," he admitted.

"Oh, did you hurt yourself?"

"No."

Hunny patted his back. She smoothed the hairs back from his face. Errl made a face.

"A little."

"Too bad. But you got away."

"Yes. We go far up into the mountains to find Hunny's Kinfolk."

"That's what you said. Do you still want to meet the airship to-morrow?"

"Oh, yes. Errl wants very much to go home."

"And Hunny?"

"Hunny Bear go home with Errl." He took her hand. Hunny nodded in human fashion.

"Will miss my Kinfolk. But this will be big adventure." Hunny loved adventures. That's why she came down from her mountain home and explored the valleys below.

"Yes, big adventure. If we find the ship. If my Teach and Pa and Mam come back for me."

"They will, Errl." Joey chewed on a blade of grass. Something crashed in the woods behind them. Joe lifted his rifle.

The black Sasquatch crouched near the trunk of a huge fir. His hands were curled into fists and his face looked terrible. Then he pitched forward.

"What's wrong?" Joey put a hand on his father's arm. Joe Locke put down the gun.

"He's shot."

"The hunters got him," Joey guessed.

"It was supposed to be me," Errl said.

"We have to help him." Hunny ran to her companion, who lay face down in the woods.

"Too late," Joe said. "Well, let them find him. Come with me, Errl and Hunny. We'll hide you in the cabin until tomorrow. With luck the hunters will think he's you, Errl."

"Like they thought I was Errl?" Hunny stroked the huge black creature.

"Wait," Joe said. He examined the body. "Bullet went clean through. Clean hole. Must have been an exploding bullet, though. Made a bigger hole coming out than going in."

"Poor Bigfoot." Joey patted Hunny's arm. "Come with us, Hunny. You can't help him and we have to hide you and Errl before the cops and hunters come back."

"This is perfect," Joe Locke said. "They'll think he's you."

"Yes." Hunny's mouth turned down and a tear trickled from her eye. "This is perfect."

Goodbye, black Bigfoot. We never fought. We didn't have to.

They turned to leave.

As they left, there came faint rustling in the dead leaves under the new fallen snow. A movement so slight they probably wouldn't have noticed it had they heard it. They walked toward the cabin.

Chapter Twenty-Eight

The white moon set before morning. Errl and Hunny slept on separate piles of blankets on the cabin floor. They woke eager to meet the day. As the sun peeked over the treetops, Errl made pictures with a pencil in a notebook to show Hunny the position of the moon and where Joe had told him the space ship would return. He pointed to the chronometer on his arm and showed where six chronos would be. He jumped up and down with excitement.

"So glad to have you back."

"Me too, Errl." She glanced at him from the corner of her eyes and ducked her head into her shoulder. She thumped him on one huge bicep.

"How you get away from the nasty humans, Hunny Bear? You said you bent the bars when the sheriff fell asleep. Is that all? Will big black Bigfoot fool the hunters, too? Are they that stupid?"

"My name is not Hunny Bear."

"Oh."

Sorry.

That's all right.

"How'd you get away, Miss No Name Bigfoot?"

"I am No Name. Very sad."

"What's your name? You must have name. Not Hunny. You have Kinfolk."

"Not tell Errl. None of his business."

"Ho ho." He bared his teeth.

"Bars in jail were bent. I bent them some more."

"I remember," he said.

"Human was sleeping at desk."

"In his chair?"

"Yes."

"I bet that was the sheriff."

"Sheriff Jeff, yes."

He wasn't sleeping, Hunny Bear. He was giving you a chance to get away.

"I was very quiet. Bars like soft mud in my hands."

"Yes. I remember. Humans so puny."

"Sheriff woke up after I left. I close door soft. Then run."

"You run good, Hunny Bear."

"I tell you something, Errl."

What?

"I don't have a name, really."

"No name?"

"No name. Bigfoot girl no name. No friends. Only hear humans when close to camp."

"How long you been here at bottom of mountain, Hunny Bear?"

"No like name Bear. That grumpy creature."

"You come with me. We give you good name. You're Hunny."

Show me more.

He drew careful diagrams on the paper with the pencil. He knew the men would come back to the cabin and they should leave right away. Joe Locke and Joey would meet them when the Earth sun swung over the top of the forest. Joe said he would.

Joe Locke always kept his word.

Hunny and Errl melted into the forest to wait for the trapper and his son.

The sun would be straight overhead at noon.

Errl was learning. He thought more about what Teach had said and checked his chronometer. It was the morning of the tenth day and four chronos.

Miles to go before they met the big ship. If it came back. If Errl was right. If Teach hadn't lied.

Teach never lied. Just like Joe the trapper and his son. He felt really good about that. He felt safe. They wouldn't lie to him. The ship would be there.

Chapter Twenty-Nine

"Ready to go, pal?" Joe Locke and Joey came back just before noon, as he said they would.

"Good thing it's winter holidays," Joey said. "I don't have to go to that dweeb school."

"Wish I had paid attention in school," Errl said.

"You had *friends* at your school. You weren't bullied."

"No. I was not bullied. Poor Joey."

"It's because of *you*."

"Yes. They think Errl is bad."

"Joey the Freak. That's what they call me. I don't want to go back."

"Joe." His father sighed and wiped the stubble on his face. "You have to go to school, son."

"I don't want to go to school, Dad. Can't I study at home?"

"I have to work and tend my traplines, Joey. You don't have anybody at home to teach you."

"Now that Mom's gone."

"Yes." His father looked sad. Joey changed the subject.

"Dad, I *really* want to go to the stars with Errl and Hunny."

"Hunny?"

"Yes. Errl said she's going with him today. I want to go, too, dad."

"It's impossible, son. I'd like to go, too. But there's no place for us on his planet."

"Yes," Errl said. "There is. You can come with me, Joey and Trapper Joe. My Mam and Pa make you welcome."

"We don't speak the language," Joe said. "No, it wouldn't work."

"We don't belong here on Earth, Dad."

"We're human, Joey. We have to stay here. The answer is no."

"Errl will think of something. Won't you?"

"I will ask Dr. Teach. He is very smart. He will think of something. Okay, Joe?"

"Okay."

The subject was dropped.

Time was like an arrow as they walked the twisted trails that led through the bush and forest. Joe Locke and Hunny knew them. Joey and Errl strode behind. Joey's short legs couldn't keep up with the Sasquatch or his dad. They often slowed down to keep pace with the boy.

"You should leave me behind."

"You go with us, Joey." Errl put a huge hand on the boy's head. "We say goodbye at the river."

"Yeah. The Mounties will be asking us questions. Pete Puffin and the sheriff might be back, too."

"Police will be here later." Joe Locke hefted his backpack. He swallowed water from a bottle that hung from his belt. "Water, Joey?"

"Thanks."

"Bigfoot go long time without water or food."

"How are your feet, Errl?"

"They fine. Bigfoot heal fast."

Joey grinned. "I wish I was a Sasquatch, Errl. I'd be big and strong like you and Hunny, could live in the woods all the time. Not just when Dad says it's okay. Not just when there's no school. I hate school."

"Why?"

"The kids make fun of me. They tell me I'm short and ugly. They tell me I think I'm so smart because I got a Bigfoot friend. They tell me I'm a freaky alien lover."

"Why that bother you, pal?"

"Are you kidding me? Wouldn't it bother you?"

"My friends make fun of Errl, too." He bared his teeth. "They pay attention to Errl. I have a best friend called Berndt. He makes fun of me, too. He does that because he likes me, I guess. I don't know why. I don't like school, either."

"You don't? You have to go to *school?*"

"Oh, yes, that's how we learn how to be smart and work in big buildings in city."

"Like your Dad?"

"Like my Pa, yes."

"What if you don't want to work?"

"I want to work. I want to be out in parks and make nice spaces for people to live."

"An architect?"

"Errl doesn't know what it's called in English, Joey. It's not what Teach does."

"What if you don't want to do *anything?*"

"Then I don't eat, I guess. Or Mam and Pa look after Errl. Or Planet X teaches Errl better. Maybe I go into army."

"There's armies on your planet?"

"Yes. Wars. Kinfolk not always get along."

"Well, that sucks."

"Why we study Earth and other planets. How to get along."

"You study us to learn how to get along? Apocalyptic."

"We take plants and medicines back. Coal and things Kinfolk need. That way no need to have wars."

"Oh, I think I see. You take coal?"

"Yes, we make very hard shiny stuff out of coal."

"Diamonds?"

"Errl not know. We use them in machines and they last long time. Nothing like that on Planet X."

"Oh, so you have wars over natural resources?" Joe Locke pulled his hat further down his forehead to block out the sun. He splashed through puddles of water on the trail. Joey noted the sun was swing-ing west.

"What chronos is it, Errl?"

"Almost five chronos."

"We're almost there."

"I tell Hunny this morning where we're going. She knows the place."

"She can lead us then?"

"Yes," Hunny said, and strode ahead. "I know all over these woods."

"Incredible," Joe muttered. "All this time I thought we were alone."

"I hear something." Errl stopped and turned his head from one side to the other, tilted his neck, then put his ear to the ground. "Many engines come this way. Dogs, too."

"Dang." Joe Locke struck his open hand with a fist. "I thought we'd get away with it for today. Just until you're safe home, Errl."

"How do we know Errl will be safe home?" Hunny asked. "And me?"

"We just have faith, Hunny." A muscle twitched in Joe's left jaw. "That's all this is. A journey of faith."

"Not faith." Errl got up and strode along happily. "Teach never lie to us."

"Maybe he can't get back."

"My Kinfolk very smart," he said. "They find a way."

"There's only you to come back for, Errl."

"Many Kinfolk will help one guy."

"Sound familiar, Joey?" The trapper heaved his backpack to a more comfortable position. He took another swallow of water. "Hmm, not much water left. River's coming up on our right, though."

"We're like the Four Musketeers, Dad."

"I was trying to teach you a history lesson, son."

"Or politics?"

"Never mind. I can tell school is over for today."

"All for one and one for all, Dad."

Errl stopped. "I got stone in my foot. Go on without me. I take stone out of foot. Then I catch up."

"No, we're not leaving you behind," Joey said. "I can hear the dogs now, and the ATVs. They're coming this way. They won't know what way we started out, but they can guess. The sheriff is a smart man. We don't want to let them catch you alone."

"The sheriff won't let them hurt us," Errl said. He began to whistle through the hair on his chin.

They stopped while he removed the pebble from his broad flat foot. Hunny waited in front, chuffing through puckered lips.

"Hunny not like to wait."

"I think she's right. We'd better hurry."

"Not six chronos yet."

"The men aren't far behind, Errl. And they've got guns and dogs."

"Tell me about school, Joey," Errl said. "I want to know."

"Me, too," Honey growled. Her voice sounded like dishes breaking in a Greek restaurant.

"Okay." Joey hefted his backpack. "It's a sad story."

Chapter Thirty

"I go to Parsnip Creek Middle School, right?"

"Right, Joey."

"I'm eleven-years-old. In grade five. Thirty kids in my class. They tease me about being a Bigfoot lover. My teacher, she took me to one side the other day. Told me to ignore them. Told me I'm a bigger person than that." He grinned. "I'm only five feet three."

Errl bared his teeth and chuckled.

"In the schoolyard I ate my lunch alone. Get on the school bus, sit alone. Big kids push me. Feel sick on bus."

"Anything good happen, Joe?" His father's mouth was grim.

"Then a new boy I never paid attention to asked if he could sit with me. I said sure. His name's Daniel. He asked me if I like Eminem. I say yeah, I got his CD. Daniel lives down the street from me, turns out. He comes over that night to listen to Eminem, and do homework together."

"Turns out Daniel's good at math." Joe Locke grinned. "Joey here's no good at math but a whiz at English lit, aren't you, Joe?"

"Yeah. So we do our homework and listen to the new CD he brought over, Sons of Granville. Awesome drummer."

Trapper Joe ruffled Joey's hair. "You got a friend, Joe?"

"Yeah, I guess so."

"You went to bed happier that night."

"Turns out next day at school Daniel's there. He has a friend, another new kid. We make a threesome, go to schoolyard and play kick the sock."

"Fun, Joey?" Errl grinned and bared his teeth. Hunny beamed.

"Yeah, we're outcasts. But in a good way, you know? Three Musketeers."

"Yeah, I know Joey." Errl stood in thought a moment. "Joey?"

"Yeah?"

"You still want to come with us on ship?"

"Oh, could I? I'd love to! I don't belong with no outcasts."

"No." Joe Locke was firm. "He can't go, Errl. Don't get his hopes up."

"I don't know if Errl can reach ship. I don't know if Hunny will go. But if Hunny can't come then I don't want to go home."

"Oh, Errl. Is it that bad?"

"Errl loves Hunny."

Hunny beamed.

"Well, let's go," Joe said. "We can't wait around for Judgment Day."

"Judgment Day? By Zorster, Errl has heard that before."

"Just a word. Means can't wait around forever."

"Thought gods and demons of Zorster were coming."

"No such thing as gods and demons." Joey hiked ahead, jaw set. His father led the way. Errl and Hunny trailed behind, taking loping but slow steps. They might be separated forever when Errl saw his ship.

If I see ship. Six chronos, Dr. Teach said. Dr. Teach is always right. Isn't he?

Chapter Thirty-One

Two Bigfoot and two humans made their way through the forest to the river. An hour later they stood on the banks of the river, overgrown with trees and shrubs. Errl stood and looked one way then the other.

"Don't know where we are," he said.

"First Nations said this is the spot," Joe replied. He checked his compass and shook his watch. "Check your chronometer, Errl."

"Not six chronos yet."

The river churned with frozen whitecaps. Hunny sat on the bank and patted the place beside her. Errl paced. Joe and Joey squatted on their heels and shared a sandwich.

"Fruit, Errl?"

"Errl eats leaves, berries and grass like Hunny."

"Good enough."

"And O-R-E-O cookies."

Hunny bared her teeth in a smile.

"Wait. Over there." Joey pointed to a circle which crushed the grass near the riverbank. "What's that?"

"That where my airpod landed!" He jumped up and down. "Thank you, Joey and Big Joe the Trapper. This is right place after all."

"It was hidden from view is all."

"My Kinfolk very smart."

Hunny turned her head. Her hearing was very keen, like Errl's. They both stood up and hugged each other.

"Errl very frightened."

"Yes, I hear it, too," Joey said after a while. It was the sound of dogs barking and the roar of ATV engines coming their way. Very close. Maybe a truck? Hunny disappeared into the trees.

"Come back," Errl called, and began to follow her. "It's almost six chronos, my Hunny Bun."

"Where'd you hear that?" Joe was amused.

"Hear it in town on TV. Man call beautiful girl Hunny Bun."

"You must be her Hunny Boy."

"No way, Joe. Gross." He hurried after the female Bigfoot.

The woods were black and yellow, deep shadows near the boles of giant Douglas firs and streaming with sunlight through the blanket of leaves far above.

Hunny? You're coming home with me?

"I'm afraid of the humans with dogs." Hunny stood almost invisible in a shaft of sunlight under a tree. "This forest used to be safe."

"Until Errl came along?"

"Yes. You spoiled the forest."

"It was never safe, Hunny. You just thought so. The Humans are not safe. Not ever."

"Joe safe. The boy is safe."

"Maybe. They want to stay here, on Earth where we are lost."

"I'm not lost on Earth, Errl. This is my home."

"You're the only one here, down off the mountain, Hunny. Errl would be lonely if Errl were only Bigfoot in world."

"Yes. I did not know better."

Now you've learned?

"You'll be lonely without Errl, Hunny. You'd have to go back to group on top of mountain, be alone again. You don't want black Bigfoot on top of mountain? He not good for Hunny. Please come with me."

"Please?"

"It a word I learned from humans. Means do what I say."

"Do what you say?"

"Please."

"Please sound better."

"Then do what I say, Hunny, please. Come with Errl."

"What is there for Hunny there on Planet X, Errl? Nobody I know. All strange food, all strange bigfoot, all strange world."

"You will learn. You'll be with me. Nothing strange. I will show you, I will take care of you and bring you to school, you'll know Teach and he will tell you how to get along on strange new world."

"Just like this one?"

"Just like this one, Hunny. You were all alone in forest, now no more alone. You won't be safe here, my golden girl."

"Because of you, Errl."

"Yes." He hung his head. He picked at a root with his toes and brought some lichen up to his mouth. He offered it to Hunny. She punched him.

"All because Hunny met Errl and my life changed."

"Yes. Errl is sorry."

Hunny pounded her chest and laughed. She sounded like a load of coal being poured into a steel bin.

"Errl is sorry. Hunny is sorry, too. Nothing will ever be the same."

"No, Hunny. Everything is changed."

"I go now."

"Where?"

Please come home with me. Say you will.

She took his hand, dark brown and golden fur together. "Maybe nothing change," she said. "Earth is like Planet X and Errl is like Hunny. All same if we're together."

"Yes." He took a deep and shuddering breath then blew his lips into a big rude sound. "All same if we're together. It still my fault," he continued.

"It still your fault," she said and tapped his shoulder. "It your fault I love you."

Far behind, the black Sasquatch followed, leaving a trail of blood. The hunters followed him.

Chapter Thirty-Two

Errl knew the black Sasquatch behind them was hurt. He worried about Hunny's friend. The Sasquatch followed, followed, thudda, thudda, thudda. The fellow stuffed the healing plants into the hole left by the bullet. He chewed as he plodded on. The blood stopped dripping from the bullet wound. His wound healed. How could that be?

Thudda, thudda, thudda

"Hey, Pete, not so fast." The hunters swerved their ATVs and trucks to avoid fallen logs and hillocks in the path. They followed the trail of blood. Then the trail of blood stopped.

"Where do we go from here?"

"They must be headed for the Oldboy River up ahead. It's about fifteen minutes from here. They're on foot. We're faster."

"We're not faster if our machines can't make it over this trail. This is rough going, Pete."

"Well, we wounded him. Not sure if there's two of them critters or not."

"He got away from Jeff twice."

"Yeah, that jail is like a tin can punched full of holes."

Someone yelled. "Mrs. Puffin?"

"I'm going back."

"You hear on the TV how this alien attacked those two birdwatchers?"

"Yeah, it was all over the news. He's showing his true colors."

"Shoot on sight, I say."

The black Sasquatch stopped about five hundred yards in front of the hunters. He hunched down under a tree. His wound had stopped dripping. He was close to the golden female and the stranger. What would he do when he reached them?

Being followed, the black fellow thought. *That's bad news for the female and the stranger.*

He scratched his head.

That's bad news for me.

Huddled behind the trunk of a fir, the Sasquatch was almost invisible. He could hear the roar of the ATVs, the churning of the sheriff's truck. He no longer left a trail of blood. They didn't know he was here, watching them go by. Every now and then a hunter would shoot a round of bullets into the dense bush.

Humans are crazy. I want to go back.

He knew now why his little group kept together high in the mountains. He wondered why the young female had joined the stranger here with the crazy gods of this world.

She must be crazy, too.

He chewed the medicine plant. He plugged the bullet hole in his shoulder. It had almost healed over.

After the humans had passed by, the Sasquatch threw back his head and howled. Errl and Hunny heard him.

"That's your friend," Errl said. "He doesn't sound hurt."

"No." Hunny hunched down in a forest of grasses. "We heal fast with grandfather's medicine plants. We know which plants to pick. He will be all right."

"He's bigger than I am."

"He's older than you, I think. You are thirteen, fourteen?"

"Yes, Hunny bun. But alien Bigfoot grow up faster than humans."

"Yes, I guessed that much." She winked at him.

"Hunny doesn't mind?"

"I like that about Errl."

They held hands. Joe Locke glanced up at the sky. "We're there."

"This path is too narrow for the ATVs and the sheriff's truck," Joey remarked.

"I wouldn't be surprised if they can blaze a trail." His father wrinkled his forehead. "I think we should maybe try to hide."

"I'm awful tired, Dad."

"I know. We'll stay here for five minutes."

Hunny beat her chest with her broad hairy fists. "Errl and Hunny will watch. We're not tired."

"Go on, then. We'll join you in a few minutes." Joe put down his pack. He offered his water bottle to his son. They all scrunched down in the tall grass. "I don't hear the engines."

"There's something else."

"Yes, I hear it, too."

The tremendous roar of a 4x4, maybe a monster truck, and the sounds of teenagers hooting and hollering.

"Help's arrived."

"If that's help, son, I'll be an elephant's grandfather."

Harriet, I've failed you and our son. Our lives are in the pockets of strangers.

Chapter Thirty-Three

The monster truck chewed to a stop on the trail.

"That your kid, Pete?"

"Heck, yeah."

The hunters all stopped their ATVs. Sheriff Jeff leaned out of his truck. "Puffin, get yer kid the heck out of here. It isn't safe for them."

"I know that, Jeff. Taylor, get yer butt outa here."

"Yee haw, Mr. Puffin."

"Yee haw, yourself. I'll dang sure shoot your truck up if you don't move it right now."

The huge wheels of the monster truck churned up mud. The teens circled the group of men, hooting and howling.

"Whatcha doing way out here, Dad? Got a Bigfoot up your butt?"

"I'm warning you, Taylor."

"Hey, Taylor, you scared of your old man?"

"Yeah, he is. Look at him run back to the truck."

"Let's go, Taylor." They all piled into the back of the truck. Rrrrrrr, the monster truck smashed through the forest. The group of men were left behind, cursing.

"That's all right, Pete. They cleared a path for us."

"Let's go, men."

"They're going to warn the Bigfoot and the trapper. I bet our wives can hear them clear back to Parsnip Creek."

"Mrs. Puffin? You still here?"

"No, she turned around a while back. Just us boys here now."

"Well, let's go. Yee haw."

The monster truck churned ahead of them, breaking the trail. The teens were not aware they helped the hunters, they were out for a good time. They didn't care about Errl and his friends, either. They just wanted to party.

Cans of Wacked Bison Sports Drink whipped into the forest. The monster truck boomed and crashed to the river. Errl and Hunny covered their ears.

"Are these our friends?" Hunny asked.

"No, they not our friends." Errl scratched his head. "I know. Ship come soon. We pretend until ship come. We pretend we're their friends."

"They're awful noisy," Joey said.

"They like to have fun." Errl bared his teeth. "We show them fun."

"How are we going to do that?"

"We play game."

He began to run along the riverbank. Hunny followed him.

"You and trapper Joe hide, young human. We lead the teens and hunters on wild duck chase."

"That's wild goose chase, Errl."

"Errl's English talk not good?"

"It's excellent, Errl. Excellent Bigfoot English talk."

The monster truck burst out of the forest. The teens hung out of every window. They hung out of the back, throwing cans of cola and *Wacked Bison Sports Drink* into the clearing. Behind them, ATVs roared. The sheriff's truck followed with the dogs in the back. Dogs howled and barked.

Joey and his father crouched in the tall grass at the side of the clearing, hearts pounding.

Errl and Hunny ran faster than the truck could churn in this bog and mud. The monster truck spun in circles in the middle of the clearing. Not far behind Errl could hear the hunters and dogs.

The teens had led the men right to the four friends where they waited in the clearing.

"Say, you know what we did?" One of Taylor's buddies scratched his head.

"What, dude? Yee haw."

"We led your old man and his hunters right to our Bigfoot pals."

"Yeah, we did that, didn't we? Sheesh. I'm sorry, buddy. Just having a good time. Thought we'd join you up there in the sky. You're looking for your friends in the flying saucer, ain't you?"

"I'm all for that, Puffin."

"My old man is going to stop them if he can."

"Yeah, with a bullet."

"I think there's a ree-ward on their heads now."

"Well, we could claim that, Taylor."

"That's not how we treat our buddies, Buster."

Gunning the engine, the truck's front tires came off the ground as the back wheels churned mud. They crashed through the forest on the other side of the clearing, lunging through the forest away from Errl and Hunny. Errl watched them go. The hunters changed course, following the noisy truck.

Hunny pounded Errl on one of his huge hairy biceps.

They're leading the hunters away from us.

"Yeah, Hunny Girl. They are."

I wonder why?

"This world is not safe. I don't wonder why anymore. But some humans are good humans."

Let's find our friends.

You mean Joe Locke and Joey?

Yes. They will come with us.

No, Hunny. Joe Locke does not want to come.

What will become of the boy and his father?

I don't know.

They circled back through the woods to the clearing again. The trucks and ATVs boomed through the forest. The noise grew faint.

It wouldn't be long before the hunters realized they'd been led on a wild duck chase. They would come back, and they'd be mad.

Hunny and Errl crouched in the grasses hand in hand. Their human friends hid near the riverbank in the shrubs. Hiding out would do no good, Joe Locke knew that. The dogs would find them and the men had weapons. He wasn't armed.

"Guns are bad things to have when people are angry or frightened," Joe Locke said. "I go hunting to get food for our freezer for the winter, that's all."

"Dad, are we gonna be all right?"

"I know the men who followed us are mad as a bear in a hornet's nest."

He feared for Errl's life. He feared for Joey.

Just then he heard a roar and felt a blast of hot wind like nothing felt before. The clearing in the shrubs where the airpod had landed was swept flat and brown. Great chunks of mud were flung up. The river boiled. At the same time hunters and dogs burst through the woods. They surrounded the clearing.

Chapter Thirty-Four

The teens in the monster truck roared back the way they had come. The trail ran through bogs, over tree roots and broken branches. Taylor knew the hunters had stopped following them. His buddies yelled and threw empty beer cans through the open window. He veered around a figure on the trail, then slammed on the brakes.

"Say, isn't that our buddy the Bigfoot?"

"Yeah, I'd say it is."

"He's black as coal dust. Not the same guy."

"Yeah, has to be. Can't be more than two of them."

"I never saw this guy before. Big as a tree. Black as Dutch licorice."

"Hop in, mister."

The big Sasquatch held his shoulder and ran into the trees. He was on his way up the logging trail to the top of the mountain. He didn't trust the noisy machine with the young humans who yelled. He didn't understand their language. He didn't trust them. It wasn't safe down here near the river. He knew the golden female would come back if she wanted to. She always did what she wanted to. She was coy. He knew he couldn't trust her, either.

The black Sasquatch held his shoulder and loped to the top of a hill. He stood and looked around. He could see the big river to the far side of the clearing. He could make out small figures on the shore. That must be the female and the stranger. There were four of them.

The Sasquatch sniffed the air. He heard *pop, pop, pop.* He knew those sounds came from what men called guns.

They were shooting at the female and her friend.

What should he do? Should he help them?

What would Grandfather Silverback do? Would he go back?

The Sasquatch held his shoulder. The wound was healed but it was sore. This land was not safe. The humans were not safe to be around.

The female had made her choice.

He turned and loped down the other side of the hill. In easy strides he crossed the forest, valley and eventually climbed the mountain to his Kinfolk.

"Taylor, if we let the cops know your dad is out here with his guns they'd come help."

"Help who, dude? The cops are just as bad as the hunters."

"No, they're not. There might be a ree-ward, too. We could try."

"Remember the last time we talked to Cranbrook station? They arrested us."

"Yeah."

"Your dad's gonna be mad."

"The sheriff's a good guy."

"There's a lot of the good ol' boys, and they've been drinking whisky, Taylor."

"I know."

"What should we do?"

"Go pick up some girls."

"Well, that's a good idea."

The truck careened into Parsnip Creek. They passed Taylor's mother, covered in mud, stuck in a bog.

"Wasn't that your mom, Taylor?"

"Yeah, guess so."

"Aren't we going to stop and help her?"

"She's pretty good at helping herself."

"What's she doing out here?"

"Think she's got a loaded rifle and come out here with Maude Barrister. They're helping Dad."

"Where's Mrs. Barrister?"

"I think she was pushing the ATV."

"Your mother *is* good at helping herself."

"Yeah, but maybe we should go back?"

"Suit yourself."

"Yeah, my mom might be real mad."

"Your dad was."

"I don't want to go home tonight, dude."

"Let's head out to Goose Lake and party, man."

"Let's pick up the girls first. I like the one with the guitar."

"They're both feisty." Taylor turned up the volume on the MP3 player in the truck. *Number three never forget by the Devil Wears Prada.* "Cool. Seen that movie?"

"Chick movie, man."

"Yeah. Apocalyptic."

The truck bounced down Main Street. Clyde Barrister stood in a lighted square of window, watching the monster truck through binoculars. That kid of Pete's was headed for trouble. Just like his dad. Nothing to be done. His wife was in the thick of it, too. He sighed. Time to fix some macaroni and cheese. He turned away from the window.

Everyone else forgot about the four friends and the hunters. It was party time.

Chapter Thirty-Five

Party time for Errl and Hunny, too. He watched as the maw of the air-pod shone a bright light to the clearing. All he had to do was get in the middle of the light and hold Hunny. They would beam up. He turned to his human friends. Joey's lower lip trembled and Joe frowned.

"Hurry," Joe said. "They're shooting at you."

"Guns can't hurt us. Dr. Teach controls the circle."

"Yes, I see the bullets drop. They don't touch us."

"Your teen friends led the hunters away. They gave us time to get ship in place."

"Yes, they're good 'uns." Joe put his arm around his son. "Hurry up, now. Take good care of Hunny, Errl. Be good."

"Errl have to be good. Mam and Pa follow Errl on big ship. Errl knows Mam and Pa would never let me be lost alone on Earth. They come back for me on ship. I know that. It part of plan if student get lost. Mam and Pa help. That Bigfoot way. They wait for me with Teach and friend Berndt. It safe there on ship. Like Joey and father, Mam and Pa love Errl."

"Were they there all along?"

"No, they would've met big ship on edge of solar system. That plan if student lost. Parents help look. Parents care and worry. Parents trust Teach but we have many ships."

"But you needed this one to beam you up?"

"We need Dr. Teach and his knowledge."

"Oh, and he's on this ship?"

"Yes. He looks out for us, me and my friends. This ship has MiddleSchool."

"Oh. Is that different from other ships?"

"Much different. Bigfoot kids go to MiddleSchool on big ship. Special ship. Special beam up and down to other planets. Special machines and books. Special teachers."

"Oh, I guess I have a lot to learn about your planet, Errl."

"Yes, Joe. Now no time."

"How will we know you're safe, Errl?"

"Teach will find a way." He bared his teeth. Hunny crouched next to him.

Are you afraid, Hunny Bun?

No, Hunny never afraid. She shivered although the air was very warm.

Are you sure you want to go with me? Black Sasquatch turned back.

I'm sure, Big Boy. Black Sasquatch very coy. Lots of girls.

Oh.

You don't believe me?

Hang on, Hunny. We're going UP.

A ring of fire blasted all around the two Bigfoot and the two humans who crouched in the clearing. The men with the guns and dogs ran away. A searchlight brighter than the first light beamed down. A rim of grass caught fire in a huge circle around the four friends. High above purred the giant spaceship closer and closer. Joey could see the screws in the door underneath the ship and the bright blue light around the door. It poured fire to keep the men and dogs away.

"Holy crow. It's your big ship, Errl. You were right all along!"

"Yes," he replied. He stood up tall and strong with his arms around Hunny. "We go home now, friend."

"No! Not without us!"

"Your father is right. You belong on Earth."

"The men are hunting us right now!"

"They all run away. Errl's friends made big noise, big fire."

"The men and dogs will be back."

"Errl will talk to Dr. Teach." He checked his chronometer. It was just past six chronos. "My Kinfolk very smart. My Kinfolk right on time."

"We found you and brought you back," Joe Locke cried. "It was meant to be, my friend."

Hunny huddled close to Errl and smacked her lips. She bared her teeth and chattered in Errl's language.

"Holy crow," Errl said. "I understand Hunny in my language."

"They must be doing something from the ship. Maybe a translator," the trapper said. "Good luck, you two. I'll never forget you."

"God bless," Joey called, something he remembered his mother had said. "May the Force be with you," he added. He wiped his eyes.

The female Bigfoot took Errl's hand and they ran together toward the bright light. A rescue airpod appeared above their heads. They were beamed up. From the Moduport in the airpod Errl could see his sister and Lally watching them. Lally smiled and made a sign of victory to him when she saw Hunny. He screamed once with joy as he rose in the sky with his golden girl. He waved both hairy arms to his friends below.

Joey and his father were trapped inside the ring of fire. The men on the other side had come back and were shooting at both the airship and their friends. A dog burst through the flames and rolled yelping on the dry ground.

Joe Locke shouted, "Sheriff, hold your fire!"

"Can't do nothing with these good ol' boys." Sheriff Jeff cupped his hands to his mouth. "Come out when the fire burns down, Joe. You and the boy won't be hurt."

"Can you guarantee that, Jeff?"

Several shots sliced through the violet tips of the flames. They fell to the ground before reaching their targets.

"Seems to me your good ol' boys had too much to drink this morning."

"What the heck is wrong with this here Remington?" Pete stood shoulder to shoulder with his hunting buddies, firing off rounds that dropped harmlessly short of the airpod and the two humans standing in the middle of the circle of fire.

"Dad, do something."

"It's okay, Joey. I got a feeling this is going to be all right."

"We let Errl and Hunny go home, Dad. We're left behind on Earth. How can it be all right? They're shooting at us and the fire is dying out. We're sitting partridges."

"I'll think of something." The trapper squinted up at the great airship. It hovered half a mile above their heads.

I made a big mistake, Harriet. I promised you I'd look after our son. I failed, sweetheart. Goodbye.

"Forgive me," Joe said.

"What?"

The flames flickered low to the ground. A dog jumped over the coals and sprinted toward them. One of the hunters cocked his rifle.

"It's hunting season," he said.

Chapter Thirty-Six

The great ship hung overhead. The airpod had docked and now held only a pilot and a couple of guards on board. They waited for the order to redeploy.

Dr. Teach was in his study in the metal humming ship. Errl took him aside. He gestured through the Moduports and danced from one foot to the other. He gibbered to Teach, half in English, half in Kinfolk language. His Mam and Pa stood by, smiling in a kind fashion at their errant son. He would do well in military school. He had learned much.

"Got to do it. Now, Dr. Teach. Please, for our Kinfolk. For me and Hunny. Must... *do it for our neighbors on Earth. Do it to end all fighting, Teach, we will learn. We can learn. I can learn, Teach, and I was...*

"Impossible."

"Yes, impossible."

He gripped the teacher by his huge hairy arm. He pointed to the ground far below, where the airpod hovered over the ring of coals, the trapper and his son.

Teach slapped Hunny on the back.

"Another student," Teach growled. "You'll be a good 'un. Got to keep Errl here in line, you know. Welcome aboard."

"What about what I said?" Errl asked. There was so little time. He tugged at Hunny's hand. Together they stood at the Moduport They looked down.

"Yeah," his best friend Berndt said. "What about that?"

"What about it?" Hunny asked.

"I'll do it." Teach sighed.

The coals burned orange, yellow, violet around the trapper and his son. They huddled together in the middle of the charred circle while the sheriff roared at Peter Puffin and his buddies to stop shooting. The dogs yipped and the bravest of them leapt the cinders, to roll burning on the ground beside Joey. The sun beat overhead, bright and benign.

"Sheriff, call off your dogs," Joe called. "We're coming out."

"Not alive, you're not." Peter Puffin growled and reloaded his Remington 700 SPS Tactical rifle.

"Pete, put that thing away."

"He's harboring a dangerous alien refugee."

"The dang alien has gone up to the sky, Peter. You can't shoot your neighbors."

"Dang right I can." *Pow Pow Pow*

"Good thing you're such a pore shot, Pete," the sheriff called. "Now put that rifle away before I have to take you in for attempted murder."

"This fire ain't no ordinary fire, Jeff. I can't get a straight shot around it. There's some kind of magnetic dee-vice up there in that flying saucer thing. I'm sure of it."

"Good thing for you there is, Pete, or you'd of killed a good friend. Now you boys put that whisky away and go on home."

The dogs howled and strained at their leashes. The flames had burned down. Spots of dry grass sprawled blackened and ruined. The hunters gripped their guns.

Joey cried, "We're too good for this world, Dad."

Peter Puffin let his dogs go. They raced over the coals and toward the man and the boy. Peter took careful aim and pulled the trigger.

Now, Teach!

A monstrous hum exploded over the forest and the ground shook and shivered. The hunters shielded their eyes. The dogs whimpered and rolled on their backs. A beam of light pierced the smoke, brighter than the sun, brighter than the flaming coals and brighter than the sky.

Joe and his son were swept up into the airpod.

"Dang!" The sheriff slapped his deputy on the back. "Nobody will ever believe us. There's nothing left but this big burned patch of ground and an empty field. Thank heaven those two boys are safe."

The airpod joined the huge metal ship. They blasted into space at the speed of light.

The men and dogs below stood near the ring of coals and stared into the empty sky. A warm wind stirred the tops of the firs.

"I never saw anything like it." Peter Puffin put down his rifle. "They're just gone. Just a red cloud left in the evening sky."

"Yeah," the sheriff said. "They were too good for this world."

Chapter Thirty-Seven

Taylor Puffin looked up. His buddies lounged around a campfire, arms around their knees. One of the two sisters by the name of Kristal strummed a plastic ukulele. Eminem played on the MP3 player. The girls sang along, mouthing the words. They fell silent.

"What is it, Tay?" His pal followed Taylor's gaze into the sky. The evening was clear.

"Is that a cloud I see?"

"A pretty strange cloud." Kristal shielded her eyes. Her sister leaned on her shoulder. Empty beer cans littered the campground. A half eaten hotdog lay forgotten in the ashes. The teens gaped and gazed upward.

"That's a jet trail."

"No, it's bigger than that. A heck of a lot bigger. Look at the top of it."

"I thought the Bigfoot said we couldn't see their spaceships."

"That's what he said."

This is a gift. From Errl's Kinfolk to yours.

"There it is. Plain as...as daybreak. A huge ship, maybe a mile up and a mile away." Taylor licked his lips.

"I'll be darned. The Bigfoot *was* from outer space."

"We met a real spaceman."

"An alien."

"We tried to turn him in. He could've probably *killed* us."

"No, he didn't seem the type."

"You're right. Not like my dad." Taylor grinned and wiped his nose. He continued to look up. The sun was setting in gold and red. The cloud formation in the sky blossomed like a bomb, like a mushroom. It was scary. From this far away they could hear a distant boom.

"This is serious stuff."

"Maybe we should get out there, make sure they're okay."

"Who? Your dad and his buddies or the aliens?"

"There was only one Bigfoot."

"No, there were two."

"Well, I think the little Bigfoot was one of ours."

"What about Joe Locke and little Joe?"

"They ain't aliens. They're friends."

"Yeah, my little brother said they trashed Joe's house."

"Oh, really? Scary stuff. Smash your little brother's Xbox."

"No, I couldn't do that. But Joey...he's all right, in my book."

"Yeah. I wonder if he'll come back? He wanted to leave with his Bigfoot friends. I bet him and his dad beamed up right in front of Puffin's face."

"What do you mean?" Kristal shielded her eyes. The ship was there one moment. Next moment it wasn't even a dot in the sky. A flash of bright light, thunder like a hundred sonic booms, and the ship was gone. Just a bright red cloud left hanging in the sky, then nothing.

They'd left.

"I'm not sure he'd want to come back," Taylor said, pulling on his lower lip with a grubby hand. "I got a feeling about that."

This is from our World to yours, Taylor. Goodbye. Joey out.

The black Sasquatch sprawled beneath the bole of a fir tree. He gazed through the frozen needles at a flash of light and a sound like distant thunder. *Goodbye, golden girl,* he thought. *I'll miss you, but not for long. There are others here on top of the mountain.*

She winked at him from the stars.

Teach stood in his study, ringed by banks of computers and purple and orange plants.

"You're home, friends."

Joe Locke took Joey's hand.

We're home.

The celebration was immense. Rockets burst across screens tuned to crazy alien jazz music. Furry creatures scampered into the room. They hugged Hunny and Errl, grappled with Joey and his father in a frenzied display of friendship. A feast sprang from the *compukitchen* especially prepared for the humans. Joey rubbed his hands in glee. The feast included a barbecue just like Mom used to fix them in the good old days. A little six legged pet much like a Cairns terrier sprang into Joey's arms and licked his face.

"I'll call him Daniel."

"You like the *zammot*?"

"He's cute. Can I keep him?"

"Sure. He belongs to the ship. Like you would say a mascot. He can be yours, Joey, if you take care of him. He needs a special friend."

"I'll take good care of him, Errl. Thanks. I really like him. I've always wanted a pet."

"He likes you, too." The six legged creature wriggled and barked. Joey put him down. He watched his new pet scamper to a bowl of biscuits in a corner of the room. He would take good care of the *zammot*.

Pa slapped Joe Locke on the back and almost knocked him over. The aliens all laughed like a forest of coconuts falling. Joe Locke hugged Mam. They looked out the Moduport at the stars. Balls of light in the sky a million times brighter than on Earth. A screen showed a picture of a vast green, pink and blue planet that waited to be discovered.

Joey breathed out in awe. His eyes were wide. He held Mam's hand.

"The wars?" He knew this ship was full of renewable energy resources and gifts.

"We'll fix it," Teach growled. "We're learning."

"So are we," Joe Locke said. "The young especially learn well."

"We can help."

Joey threw back his head, mouth open. There on the screen, on the alien planet, was a group of humans. They dug in a garden with their children. Beside them aliens who looked like Errl and Hunny helped with the planting. Other humans lounged in front of grass huts in the distance.

"What's that?" Joey's eyes were drawn especially to a group of people, kids included. "Who are they? I thought we'd be alone here, Dad."

"They asked to come with us many years ago. On each trip, there's always a few humans who want to leave Earth behind," Teach explained. "They live in peace. They teach us much and we teach them. Soon there will be no wars. We learn to get along. We learn much from the humans and they learn from us."

"Awesome." Joe wiped a tear from his eye. In one of those family groups was a place for him and his son. *Harriet. Goodbye, sweetheart. I'll always remember you. Wish me well on this brave new world.* After proper introductions had been made to the humans, they all tucked into the feast.

Hunny smiled at Errl's best friend Berndt. Berndt gazed back at Hunny. They burped.

She was always coy.

Mam and Pa, brown furry creatures eight feet tall, held hands. Errl shrugged and popped a gummy wad into his mouth. He chewed and threw his head back. He laughed like a dozen bowling balls dropped on a tin alley.

He was going home.

About the Author

Kenna McKinnon is a Canadian freelance writer and self-employed medical transcriptionist, runner, volunteer, sporadic student of hatha yoga, karate and kickboxing, and frequent walker. She lives in a high rise bachelor suite in the trendy neighborhood of Oliver in the City of Edmonton. Her most memorable years were spent at the University of Alberta, where she amazingly graduated with a degree in Anthropology (1975). She has lived successfully with schizophrenia for many years and is now a senior woman, member of the Writers' Guild of Alberta and the Canadian Authors Association. She had three wonderful children and three grandsons.

Kenna is the author of *SpaceHive*, a middle grade sci-fi/fantasy novel traditionally published by Imajin Books; *The Insanity Machine*, a self-published memoir with co-author Austin Mardon, PhD, CM, including the latest research available at the time of writing; and *DISCOVERY – A Collection of Poetry*, all released in 2012. Her books are available in eBook and paperback worldwide on Amazon, Smashwords, Barnes & Noble, and selected bookstores and public libraries. *BIGFOOT BOY: Lost on Earth* is Kenna's newest MG/YA novel, released by Mockingbird Lane Press, a traditional small press.

Her author's blog: http://kennamckinnon.blogspot.com/
Twitter: @KennaMcKinnon
Facebook: KennaMcKinnonAuthor
Goodreads:
https://www.goodreads.com/author/show/6480104.Kenna_McKinnon

Made in the USA
Columbia, SC
10 March 2020

88958649R00088